WINTER TALES

Winter and its festivals, celebrated alike by Orkney's Stone-Age builders and their Christian successors, predominate in this collection of short stories by George Mackay Brown who looks at the effect of new ways of thinking and working on the ancient patterns of Orkney life. Christmas was a time for telling stories round the hearth fire and the author and his island community are part of that living tradition. He values it and engages in it, a story-teller for all seasons, transforming everything by passing it, as Seamus Heaney has put it, 'through the eye of the needle of Orkney'.

WINTER TALES

To Jackie

WINTER TALES

by

George Mackay Brown

Magna Large Print Books
Long Preston, North Yorkshire,
England.

British Library Cataloguing in Publication Data.

Mackay Brown, George
    Winter tales.

    A catalogue record for this book is
    available from the British Library

    ISBN 0-7505-1090-0

First published in Great Britain by John Murray (Publishers)
Ltd., 1995

Copyright © 1975, 1989, 1990, 1991, 1992, 1993, 1994, 1995
by George Mackay Brown

Cover illustration © Nathalie by arrangement with Allied
Artists

The right of George Mackay Brown to be identified as the
author of this work has been asserted in accordance with
the Copyright, Designs and Patents Act, 1988

Published in Large Print 1997 by arrangement with John
Murray Ltd.

Magna Large Print is an imprint of
Library Magna Books Ltd.
Printed and bound in Great Britain by
T.J. International Ltd., Cornwall, PL28 8RW.

Contents

Acknowledgements

'The Paraffin Lamp' was first published in *Hydro Electric Magazine* (1975); 'The Laird's Son' (1989), 'A Boy's Calendar' (1990), 'The Woodcarver' (1991), 'Ikey' (1992) and 'The Architect' (1993) were first published in *The Scotsman;* 'The Children's Feast' (1989), 'The Lost Sheep' (1990), 'Three Old Men' (1991), 'A Nativity Tale' (1992) and 'St Christopher' (1993) in *The Tablet;* 'Shell Story' was first published in *Xanadu,* U.S.A. (1993); and 'The Sons of Upland Farm' in the *Daily Telegraph* (1994).

Foreword

It was in winter that the islanders gathered round the hearth fire to listen to the stories.

Harvest was gathered in. The ears that had listened only to necessary farming and fishing words all the year of toil and ripening were ready for more ancient images and rhythms.

A tongue here and there was touched to enchantment by starlight and peat flame.

Then the whole twelvemonth from Candlemas to Twelfth Night was celebrated, in story and music.

Going over tales I've written during the last decade or so, I was not too surprised to see that many of them are calendar tales, that yield their best treasure in midwinter when the barns are full.

The mystery of light out of darkness has been with us since the builders of Maeshowe five thousand years ago. The Celtic missionaries gave the mystery breadth and depth.

I like to think I am part of that tradition.

Much of the old story-telling has withered before the basilisk stare of

9

newsprint, radio, television. Maybe, the people reckoned, after 1873, it was better to forget the ancient sorrows and joys. There had been too much hardship. The promised land lay all before them.

But not many modern stories hold children from play, and old men from the chimney corner.

Every community on earth is being deprived of an ancient necessary nourishment. We cannot live fully without the treasury our ancestors have left to us.

Without the story—in which everyone living, unborn, and dead, participates— men are no more than 'bits of paper blown on the cold wind...'

10

The Paraffin Lamp

I can still see him, coming home from the peat-hill in his cart long after the other farmers had taken their peats home by tractor or lorry. He did have a tractor, but most of the time it rusted in the shed. His horse Sammy was the last horse on the island. It worked for him, and he was kind and patient with it, for as long as the creature had strength to plough or cart. Once it began to fail, he would not tolerate suggestions that it ought to be shot. Sammy had been his friend and fellow earth-worker for twenty years and more. He tended it with great gentleness till the last breath was out of its once-powerful body. Then he dug a deep grave for Sammy. A few of the neighbours came to help with the burial. They saw the old man's mouth moving while the first clods were being kicked and shovelled in; and they thought it sounded like a prayer or a piece of a psalm.

He took them back to the croft house and poured out a bottle of whisky for the buriers (you could hardly call them mourners).

He was a man who lived entirely in the past. He disliked all the fruits of progress that his fellow-islanders were beginning to splurge in: motor cars, wireless sets, gramophones, bakehouse bread, Edinburgh beer.

One morning the good-wives in every farm and croft turned a tap, and out gushed sparkling water, for the first time. What an improvement that was! The old man went on taking his two pails to the well on the side of Wilderfea.

'Now, Thomas, look here,' said the minister one day when he was visiting, 'this won't do at all! Your life would be very much easier if you marched with the times. Can't you see that? What's wrong with a wireless set? Next time I'm at the Presbytery meeting in Kirkwall I'll get you one cheap, for a few pounds—I know a place. How fine it is to hear the news, and the weather forecast, and Scottish dance music... And that hearth over there, and the iron chain for hanging your pots and kettle on—man, Thomas, the women here are never done praising their stoves—what a change it's made in their lives... If you had running water, too, what a lot cleaner you could get your shirts, and your bed-clothes and everything.'

There was silence for a while on each side of the hearth. The old man seemed

12

to be considering the minister's advice. He said, after a while, that the worst thing that had happened in the kirk in his time was when they started singing man-made hymns in place of the psalms of David. Could the minister not raise that matter at the next Presbytery meeting in Kirkwall?

The minister rose, and pressed the old rough rheumaticky hand, and went away with a sigh.

As soon as he was gone, the crofter lit his pipe and looked under the bed for a bottle of ale.

The next thing to go down under the march of progress was the tilley lamp. They had hissed and glared on every farm dresser for twenty winters and more. In a month or two, electricity was to come to the island. The electricians from the town had a busy time of it, wiring every house for the great switch-on. The wives bought cookers, irons, radios, toasters, fan-heaters, fires. (A few even went so far as to enquire about refrigerators.)

That spring the old man fell ill, with influenza or some other infection. He had been failing slowly, of course, for years. With great reluctance he accepted the kindly offer of Josh Heddle to plough out his field with the tractor. (It was as though a machine would somehow desecrate his

13

acres.) And one day in late summer, when the old man was slowly recovering from his illness—but still not able to smoke his pipe—Josh stood in the door and said he had just finished cutting the old man's harvest; and it was a good crop. The old man thanked Josh. Then he reached up to a tea-caddy on the mantelpiece and opened it and took out a roll of notes and gave Josh five pounds. (That was where he kept his wealth—he didn't trust banks.)

Then, a week later, he had a relapse. 'This is the end of him,' said the islanders. 'Poor old Thomas.' They carried him down to the pier on a stretcher and shipped him to the hospital in Kirkwall. While he was away, the minister and a few others decided that, if he was ever to come back, the old man could not go on living in the same conditions of hardship. 'We will do nothing rash,' said the minister. 'We will not overwhelm him all at once with the benefits of science. But it's time that old paraffin lamp was done away with—impossible to read by it—dangerous too, if he was to knock it over. Thomas—if he comes home—will come home to a bright electric bulb in the ceiling...'

Thomas did come home, after a month, at the start of winter. He had fought off the illness—some of the dark power

14

of the earth, hoarded slowly over many generations, was still in him. He thanked the islanders for all their kindness to him. He thanked them for the pear-shaped opaque thing hanging from his ceiling. So that was what electric light was like? John Heddle switched it on—the interior of Biggingdale had never been so bright...

That evening, when the minister went along to see how the old man was after his journey, he found him reading *The Pilgrim's Progress* by the dim light of the paraffin lamp. He was very pleased to see the minister. He said that was a very handy thing, the electric light. He could see by it to fill his old lamp, and trim the wick, and light it with a wisp of straw from the fire.

Lieutenant Bligh and Two Midshipmen

Bligh of the Bounty *had a young Orkney midshipman, George Stewart, who took no active part in the mutiny but returned to Tahiti on the* Bounty *with the mutineers, to his native 'wife' by whom he had a daughter, Peggy.*

Midshipman Stewart surrendered to the Pandora *and was drowned when that ship foundered on the Great Barrier Reef, on the voyage back to Britain.*

Bligh says of Stewart in his account of the mutiny that he 'was of creditable parents in the Orkneys, at which place, on the return of the Resolution *from the South Seas in 1780, we received so many civilities, that in consideration of these alone I should gladly have taken him with me...'*

A ship's carpenter with an Orkney name, Peter Linklater, accompanied Bligh on the launch that was set adrift from the Bounty *and reached Timor after a piece of superb navigation.*

George Stewart became the hero of Byron's poem The Island.

This story is about the first meeting of Bligh and Stewart, at a house in Hamnavoe.

16

On the return of HMS *Resolution* from the South Seas expedition—during which Captain Cook was killed—the ship anchored in the harbour of Hamnavoe in Orkney, under the command of Lieutenant William Bligh, to take aboard fresh water at Login's Well.

Two Hamnavoe merchants, Mr Spence and Mr Stewart, allowed themselves to be rowed out to the ship. They were civilly received by two of the officers, who opened a bottle of claret and drank with them. The young officers regretted that Lieutenant Bligh was not available that morning; he had much book-work to do at his desk.

The Hamnavoe merchants said they were well aware of their temerity in interrupting the work of such a great and important vessel. They commiserated with the officers, after the second glass of claret, upon the untoward death in a savage distant place of the great Captain Cook.

Mr Stewart, endeavouring to conceal his uncouth northern accent by the use of acceptable English, said that he would esteem it a high honour indeed if the captain of this fine ship, along with the officers, would accept an invitation to dine with him on the following evening, at his unworthy house. 'There it stands, all in its own green yard on the side of that

17

steep hill. It would indeed be the greatest honour to him and to all his house...'

Mr Spence smiled too, and nodded, and put down his glass. His house was down at the waterfront, and had fish smells.

The young officers offered to broach another bottle—were refused, with smiles and uplifted palms—they had their businesses to attend to, the Hamnavoe merchants, stores and workers to be overseen.

But the officers agreed to acquaint Mr Bligh with the invitation, and no doubt the gentlemen would be hearing from Mr Bligh before sundown.

With smiles and courtesies, the local big-wigs were seen down to their waiting dinghy, and rowed to the stone jetty at Ness, by Tomison the boatman, who had a filthy clay pipe sticking upside down out of his beard.

All this was closely observed from houses and piers and taverns—windows that overlooked the harbour and the great furled visitant: and uncomplimentary remarks were made by this old sailor and that concerning the fawners and creepers who would not so much as deign to speak to the likes of them, who had as much honest salt in their blood and bones as those pressed dockside men who laboured on the king's ship.

'Oh,' said Lieutenant William Bligh to one of those duty officers, 'I'll go ashore. I'll go to the man's house. Stewart? Mr Stewart—I'll visit him. That is the house there, on the steep side of the bay? Take a letter to Mr Stewart. I'll write a letter. Where's that boy Brisco? It will be a pleasure to look through a window and see green fields. Do you reckon he keeps a good larder, this Mr Stewart? Oh, no matter, but a side of fresh mutton...James, here you are. James Brisco, I want you to write a letter for me. I am tired of pens and ink-horns and papers, James. Sit well in at the desk, man. Are you ready? Well, this. Good writing now, James. No blots, no foolish flourishes. Charge the quill. "Lieutenant William Bligh of HMS *Resolution* presents his compliments to Mr Stewart of the White House in..." What is the name of this wretched village, James? Hamnavoe. One of those damned foreign-sounding names, Irish or Danish—spell it how you will. Do you think this Stewart might chance to have a fair pretty daughter, James? It may be. Therefore, James, in hope that you may prove a gallant gentleman to Miss Stewart, you will accompany me to this dinner at the White House. Spruce yourself, James, powder your wig, brush your lapels. Now, where were we?..."in Hamnavoe, and will be pleased to avail himself of Mr Stewart's hospitable invitation to dinner tomorrow evening at 7 o'clock, together with Mr James Brisco, midshipman"...I think that will do. No need to sign the thing. I am tired of writing my name. I wonder if the man expects an invitation in return, on board *Resolution?* It does not necessarily follow. Much depends on the beauty or otherwise of Miss Stewart, eh, James, if you had a say in the matter... It could be, James, that there are several Miss Stewarts, five or six. How foolish of Jarvis not to enquire after Mr Stewart's family, as to their number and sex. The man is invincibly ignorant. There may have to be a supper on *Resolution.* There may be. I cannot promise.'

'Sir.'

'Yes?'

'The men request shore leave, within limits.'

'What? Certainly. When have I ever denied them? In companies of twelve, six hours ashore, beginning at noon. A responsible seaman in charge of each party. I want no drunkenness, no fighting, no disrespect to the local women. Or I shall know the reason. They will answer for it, James.'

'Sir.'

'Tell Mr Andrews to keep a shrewd eye

open. If there should be a boatyard or a carpenter's shop. What *Resolution* badly needs is a good carpenter. I swear the woodwork is all warped and wormeaten since Kelly died, may the waves wash kindly over him, the poor man. It was a joy to watch Kelly with saw and plane. He sickened on us. Tahiti. A jaundice. If there should be a good carpenter in that wretched village, and he willing. Let the bosun look about him too.'

'A dozen men, sir, and six hours' leave.'

'Yes, James Brisco, and they are to have a shilling each. No, there is no need to seal the letter. Well, yes, perhaps. The Misses Stewart will be the more impressed, looking at a red seal. You fool, James, you'll burn your fingers!'

Lieutenant Bligh and Midshipman Brisco dined at the White House more agreeably than they had expected. There was baked trout, lamb chops, and a great roasted haunch of beef. And also—what they had not expected—a bowl of fruits: oranges, French apples, and Jamaican bananas.

'Many vessels sought anchorage here, Sir, in the westerly gale last weekend, I assure you, Sir, from all latitudes,' said Mr Stewart.

Lieutenant Bligh drank only water. James Brisco tasted with relish every glass that was set before him: sherry, the burgundy and hock, the glowing rich port, and (having dabbed the last of the grease from his lips) the local whisky. Bligh sought the midshipman's eye more than once: to no avail. James's eye was cast down demurely, on glass or plate, or set smilingly on the face of Mrs Stewart, or teasingly into the blushing starry-eyed face of Miss Stewart.

Alas, Elizabeth Stewart was aged only twelve. There was another Miss Stewart, well over sixty, a sister of the host. 'A sensible good woman,' said Bligh afterwards.

There was a young man, the son of the house, called George, who sat and said nothing, or mumbled this and that of small consequence, much to his father's displeasure. 'Don't mumble, man. Speak clear and true. When you go to sea, you'll have to shout into gales. Is that not so, Mr Bligh?'

So, the son of the house was to be a sailor: in command, at last, of one of his father's ships, no doubt. They had not been long in the house till they were acquainted with the fact that Mr Stewart together with other Orkney gentlemen had three ships that traded with Scandinavia, and into the Baltic.

Mr Bligh said that indeed a good strong voice was an asset on the bridge of a ship.

'It is just that George is going through an awkward stage,' said the aunt. 'I'm sure, when he was a boy, he had as clear and merry a voice as was to be heard. With the first sharpening of the razor come confusions and hesitancies. I have no fears for George. He will make as good a sailor as ever stood between sun and sea. Pour yourself a little of that burgundy, boy. It'll make you bold.'

George looked as if he wished himself a thousand miles away, in some Pacific isle, perhaps.

Yet his ordeal was not over. They would speak about him still. He swallowed a mouthful of roast beef, only half chewed.

'And yet,' said Mr Stewart gravely, 'that is not the kind of sailor I would wish the boy to be. I would wish him to be of service to his country, sir. An honourable career untouched by trade, the sweat of copper and silver, the kind of career such as you yourself follow, sir, and young Mr Brisco. This is the kind of sailor I would wish George to be.'

'He has good skill in navigation,' said Miss Stewart. 'The old sailors say so, and they don't praise easily.'

'Yes,' said James Brisco to Elizabeth, 'and I am going to carry you on board ship this very night, will-you nill-you, and you are to sail with us as far as Virginia

23

and New Holland. Orkney you shall not see until seven years are come and gone.'

Elizabeth stuffed her handkerchief into her mouth and half choked with mirth. She threw herself back in her chair with a wild gust of merriment, until a cold glance from her father sobered her a little. But not for long.

'It is certain,' said Mr Brisco. 'I do assure you.'

Elizabeth pushed aside her plate—she had eaten no more than a bird—and put her head down on the table and her whole body shook.

'It must be so,' said the midshipman gravely. 'Perhaps Brazil, too.'

So, thought Bligh, our host grows ashamed of the modest ladder near whose top rung he now stands. This is becoming common everywhere. Sweat of silver, indeed! As if only an inferior sort of man were required for trade and commerce. Ah, what might not Mr Stewart have become—in his own opinion—had he had the opportunity to immerse himself in his youth in the classics! He would have been as good a gentleman as any, he. The whole of society operates on this yearning towards a higher excellence for oneself and one's family and, in the case of these merchants, for one's class—even here, among these barren uttermost isles.

Society is a machine of large cogs and small cogs. It must be liberally lubricated with the oil of yearning-for-betterment. *I am as good a man as he, given the opportunity.* That is the attitude of so many of those new merchants, both wealthy and those operating still just above the level of the poverty they had risen from but lately (like this Stewart) and liable at any time—should their ships and cargoes come to grief and wreckage—to sink back into the original hunger and dirt. And, unspoken naturally, *Had my George had Mr Brisco's advantages, he might prove the better midshipman...* It might come to this, that certain privileged ground might have to be yielded to those who sweated gold and silver, by the ancient landed families. The better sort, a careful selection of them, might have to be admitted to political power, into society and the universities and His Majesty's armed services: the upper echelons of the 'goldsweaters'. But would the process stop there? Below Mr Stewart and the merchants and petty traders, and such worthy craftsmen as shipwrights and ostlers and scriveners, were the teeming masses of the toilers, hewers of wood and drawers of water, the undisciplined hordes of agricultural workers and industrial workers. If they were to discover discontents with their honest lowly estates, and find men to organise their dark dangerous energies, what might happen then in society? Pooh, he was letting himself drift a little on the tide of his idle fancies! Such forces could be safely contained, so truly and firmly established was the structure of the state. History showed a few revolts and mutinies from the inarticulate masses, but the smoulderings had been quickly stamped out. A few adjustments of the machine, now and then, obedient to social and economic pressures, and the state once again operated well enough. Not perfectly—there being no such thing as perfection on this earth, as regards the affairs of men; but adequately. A ship-of-war: now there was a great state in microcosm. Let but all do their prescribed work adequately and with a good heart, and life on shipboard would move as if to music. He thought with affection of the common seamen of *Resolution*. They were good men and he felt affectionately towards them. With discipline and kindliness, such as obtained on a well-ordered ship, much may be made of those whose lives had been sunk hitherto in wretchedness and ignorance. There is good in all men, from the lowest to the highest. Indeed, in his experience, an honest poor sailor had more to be said for him than such fops as Andrews and Jarvis, sons of clergymen both.

Bligh was aware of a silence at the table, and of his name being uttered. 'Mr Bligh,' Mr Stewart was saying, 'would you please to move into the next room? There is a harpsichord. I've persuaded my daughter to give us a half-hour of music. She plays with taste, though I say it myself.'

The hostess—poor faded silent woman— and the two female servants had removed the plates, cutlery, and decanters into the kitchen. Only the great bowl of fruits stood in the centre of the polished walnut table.

The men moved into the drawing room, and young Elizabeth trailed after them—after James Brisco, rather, right on his heels—a sweet-smelling shadow.

'Now, my girl,' said Mr Stewart, 'you will play for us. There are the new sheets of Haydn. Have you tried them out?'

Elizabeth nodded. She sat down at the stool. She turned a new crisp sheet of music.

'No,' cried James Brisco, 'I think she should not play. It will be too much. It will melt my heart, I know it. It will unman me, should she play. I will weep like a child.'

Elizabeth was on the verge of new laughter. Her head drooped over the keyboard. Never had she endured such exquisite teasing. She had not thought such enchantment to be in the sombre practical race of men—and this particular man so young and so handsome, like a prince out of a fairy tale.

'I shall play presently,' she said, 'once I have chosen a suitable piece.'

Mr Stewart, having filled his long pipe with tobacco, set it on the mantelshelf and hastened to open the decanter on the sideboard.

'This is our very own whisky,' he said. 'Made and distilled in this very village. The excisemen have not set their seal to it. They see frail smoke now and then, on a calm day, among the hills. But the stills are so well hidden that they rarely find one.'

Bligh declined a glass. 'I think,' said he, 'you should not offer more liquor to Mr Brisco. Mr Brisco has done well enough with your wines.'

'Indeed I will have a glass,' cried James Brisco. 'Fill it up to the brim, Mr Stewart. I have not tasted whisky in my life.'

Bligh had never heard such insubordination. The boy was drunker than he thought. He threw a sombre glance at James Brisco: but James Brisco was bent over Elizabeth and the keyboard. He turned a sheet of music. The girl still sat, her hands in her lap.

Young Mr Stewart had shaken his head at the proffered glass of whisky; Bligh was glad to note that. George Stewart had been very moderate at table also: one glass of red wine, one of white, no more.

The host was inviting Bligh to stand at the window that overlooked the harbour, the fishing-boats, and the great furled ship. There were things he wished to say in confidence.

Bligh had had enough of the man, his self-satisfaction, his sycophancy, his snobbery. Yet, out of courtesy, they could not leave the house for another half-hour at least.

It was young George Stewart that his father wanted to talk about; that much was obvious. The man was flushed in the face; he too had drunk too much; more than he was accustomed to. 'I have only this son and another,' he was saying. 'I have ambitions for this one. If a word was put in on his behalf, in the correct quarters, do you not think...' Bligh had heard it all before, many times: from country squires, parsons, ladies of quality, shipowners, lawyers. Could he see his way, possibly, to get this son or that nephew or cousin entered into the service? It would be a matter of the most deep gratitude and obligement. The young man (so went the tale always) was wasting his time—taking up with bad company, gamblers and hell-rakers—there was good in him, if only some order and discipline were to be put upon his life, such as in His Majesty's ships-of-war. This favour, of course, would not be sought without some recompense... He let the wind of Mr Stewart's ambitions blow itself out, which it would do presently, only half listening to this Orcadian variation on the theme. Meantime he eyed the subject of the monologue.

George Stewart was a well-favoured young man. There was no doubt about that. His modesty when his name had been under discussion recommended him to Bligh, and also his temperance with regard to drink. A young man's eyes conveyed much to Bligh; there was a steadiness of purpose in young Stewart's, and a sense of outwardness and questing: but this only manifested itself now and then, when his eyes glanced momentarily to the window, going beyond the silhouettes of the sailor and the merchant, to the great ship, the harbour, and the islands of Scapa Flow. Mostly his eyes were veiled and dreamy, as if he was content meantime with the inner landscape; where upon the soul's tree that is already budded and beginning to tremble with life, the soul sits furled and waiting: for that far summons that is part of the estate of every man born.

The young man had been embarrassed and awkward over dinner. Here he seemed to be at peace with himself, and quite oblivious to the other occupants; his young sister, her hands poised sometimes over the keyboard and sometimes tucked together in her lap, while the half-tipsy young midshipman cajoled and rallied her like a travelling showman—and the grave officer and the garrulous father (he half-tipsy also) pleading a case.

More and more Bligh found himself preoccupied with the silent solitary young man—though, having long experience of studying men from his secret eyrie, he gave little outward sign of it. Bligh's ear, slightly dulled by time and the infinite music of all the oceans, seemed intent on what his host was saying. Now the man had moved to a new tack: he and his family might not be what they appeared to be, by any means. The name 'Stuart' or 'Stewart' was not a common name in the Orkneys; most of the names here were of Norse origin. No: Stewart was a Scottish name, and if one paused to think about it for a moment, the most illustrious, the most high-born name of all, that borne by the royal family of Scotland, that talented ill-starred family whose scions—Mary Queen of Scots, King Charles I, Prince Charles Edward—were

31

'like trumpet-calls of tragedy'. The man used those very words, as if he had rehearsed them to himself secretly many a time, testing them and relishing them on his tongue; and now, being slightly flown with drink, he could articulate them aloud. What would come next?

George Stewart, from the fireplace, threw at his father an irritable contemptuous glance, and then returned to his private thoughts, which increasingly intrigued Lieutenant Bligh: for the young man stirred memories and hopes in himself that he had thought long dead, until this evening not even a rustle of dry leaves about the cobbles.

The host babbled on. The royal Stuarts of Scotland had, two centuries since, sent a shoot of themselves north to Orkney—not, of course, of the direct line; but a natural son of King James V, Robert Stewart, had been set up in Birsay as Robert, Earl of Orkney, and in Birsay he had built himself a sumptuous palace—now, alas, somewhat dilapidated.

And this Robert Stewart, in his turn, had infused tinctures of the blood royal here and there in Orkney—not too squanderously, oh no, but there were a few of the better sort of family in this part of the kingdom that could, with a certain degree of certitude, claim kinship. Earl

Robert Stewart had been half-brother to Mary Queen of Scots herself.

Ah, thought Bligh, this was it: let Bligh not think he was dealing with a low peasant who had with a measure of cunning managed to climb up into the ways of business. By no means: Bligh was talking to a man who might be more nobly descended than himself. But now, that having been established, they could deal with each other on a more or less equal footing.

Young George Stewart, from over by the fireplace, murmured, 'Stewart is also the name of a well-known travelling family, tinkers...'

The father, caught up in the high stream of his thoughts, seemed not to have heard. The 'Stewarts of Burray, the Stewarts of Hoy, the Stewarts of Stromness...' on and on he babbled.

Meantime the child at the harpsichord had consented to play. But either because she had no talent for music, or because the presence of James Brisco bending over her was too distracting, she made sorry work of the few bars she essayed. 'Ah,' said James Brisco, 'you play exquisitely, you have the true touch, you little island muse...' But the girl knew better. Her fingers faltered above the thrumming keys. She looked imploringly up at the young sailor, as

33

if to say, 'Please go away. No, don't go away, I beg you. But stop teasing me. Stop throwing the enchantment of your shadow across my sheet of music.'

'Once again,' said James Brisco, and pulled one of the little fair curls over her ear. 'Next time the music will flow like a stream, a pure surge from beginning to end.'

Elizabeth's head drooped.

George Stewart left the fireplace. He walked over and stood at the south window, looking out. Lieutenant Bligh could see only his profile. The young man's gaze was directed towards the blue hills of Hoy and at the westward-seeking current of Hoy Sound, a powerful thrust of water that mingled further out with the Atlantic Ocean. A sash of the window had been opened a little, for the evening was mild. From far off, murmurous, many-voiced, incessant, came into the drawing room the music of the great sea.

He had gone over there, the boy, to rid himself of the imbecile chatter of his father and the pathetic plinking of his sister. He stood there, still and quiet, absorbed in the mighty elemental harmony.

The merchant had left the theme of his possibly royal descent and (having filled James Brisco's glass and his own from the decanter, excusing himself meantime for

34

the breach in social continuity) had moved on to more practical matters. Though he was by no means a wealthy man—oh no, such an idea would be laughable—yet, if his son were to get some kind of footing in the world of great affairs, a humble footing, he (Mr Alexander Stewart) was not lacking the means to see that the boy was well furnished with the necessary gear and appurtenances and financial backing; George would not go into society in rags and patches, with salt in his ears and barley-husks in his hair. By no means. For, besides his partnership, three ships, and connections in Leith, Bergen, Gothenburg, he owned, in whole or in part, thus and thus property, namely, Massater in South Ronaldsay and...

While the tipsy man babbled on, Bligh studied the profile of the young sailor-merchant over by the window. There, but for the ordinance of God, stood he thirty years ago and more, with all adventure before him. The tree shaken with sap, the buds yearning to open and unfold, desire and beauty and song everywhere. Every delight seemed possible then, there was little or nothing beyond the reach of young strength and young endeavour and young ambition. The horizon beckoned. The time had come to put aside childish things. It was springtime, April: time to become a part of the marvellous brave saga of man.

Ah, it had turned out otherwise, grievously otherwise. But do your duty—he had been told, and so he had believed—and all these other delights of life will be added unto you: joy and solace of love, the doors that wealth and property can open, honour and fame, the approbation and comradeship of one's peers, the respect and trust of inferiors, skill at the trout-stream and in the hunting-field, high courtesy in drawing rooms, tables, dance floors.

With a single-minded devotion he had devoted himself to duty, from midshipman on, to the proper and true and scrupulous performance of those tasks which had to be done. And they had been well done; he himself was in no doubt about that, and his superiors nodded grave approval, and advanced him—very slowly, it was true, but that was in the very nature of the service, a man had to prove his worth over and over again, beyond any question, before he was offered a higher responsibility. There were rare exceptions, like that reckless hot-headed Nelson, who impressed even in this time of peace by a kind of excess imagination translated into immediate action; and that flair, from time to time (it seemed) impressed their lordships at the Admiralty, often against their better judgement. Sailors like Nelson were in love with death: all that came between such men and the dark door of the beloved must be tasted with a wild extravagant delight, for the time was short, and the bride of silence was waiting.

Such had not been Bligh's way. Everything to be done had been considered and executed with the slow skill of the accomplished journeyman.

He looked, and it seemed to be good. But not all was good: the promise of youth does not flower, at least as one expects. True, he had married his Betsy and he cherished the daughters she had borne him. But he could never free himself from his rather humble origins: the son of a customs officer. 'Thus high,' decreed their lordships of Admiralty, 'for the common sort, and no higher.' He had made of himself a stern accomplished unloved officer. That he would remain until he withered, and his story but a few chiselled words on the stone of a country churchyard: the words themselves, over centuries, weathering and ghosting to an indecipherable blank.

So Bligh considered, without bitterness, absorbed in the profile of the young man who listened, head tilted sidelong into hand, to the increasing music of the Atlantic. For now, as always near sunset, the harp-strokes, the lingering flutes, the muted drums of ocean, seemed to proliferate.

What would be the future of this young man? Would he deal in 'the sweat of silver' and bonded cargoes and bills-of-lading until he grew at last into a true son of his father, an ageing bore and windbag? God forbid. For all his silence and seeming surliness, there was something of great promise in George Stewart. He was standing now (to alter the image) on the same shore that William Bligh had stood on thirty odd years before, in the first of the flood, poised and waiting. But, beyond a doubt, life would be different for this boy: the very poise of his head, his eager stance over by the window, forbade any replication of his father or of his father's career. With a slight movement back from Mr Stewart, so that he could bring more of the boy's face into his view—but without seeming to—Bligh noted the deep melancholy and the brimming sensuousness of his expression. Here was another who was in love with death. To such a one, on his brief voyage, life offered her gifts in abundance.

At that moment the boy turned his face and looked full into the face of Bligh.

It was like the mysterious mingling of two oceans.

Bligh smiled. The boy's full lips parted,

his eyes had a look of candour and challenge and great sweetness. Then he turned back to the sea sounds.

A first star shone through the pane above his head.

Mr Stewart babbled on and flushed his teeth once more with whisky, till a drop or two dribbled down his chin.

And now, over by the harpsichord, a little drama took place. Elizabeth had ventured upon the sonata twice more, with singular unsuccess. James Brisco bade her, 'Be brave! Be undismayed! Be careless as a bird. Now, once more, my little sweetheart...'

The girl got to her feet, sent the stool on to the floor behind her with a clatter, and stumbled with a wail and a sob towards the door. And there, as if she had been waiting outside all this while, her aunt stood in the open doorway and gathered the girl (whom first infatuation had reduced to a state more wretched than any childhood misery) to her, bending and nestling the inconsolable head to her, whispering good words. Then, with a shake of her head at the men inside, Miss Stewart took Elizabeth's hand and led her out of the room and closed the door gently behind her.

'Tut-tut!' said Mr Stewart, 'childish nonsense. You are not to distress yourself,

Mr Brisco. Your pardon, Mr Bligh.'

'I shall comfort myself with another drink, if I may,' said James Brisco.

George Stewart did not stir from his post at the window.

'Put down that decanter, sir!' cried Bligh. James Brisco, startled, let the decanter down with such force that the grey whisky swirled and washed about inside it for a full minute.

'Mr Stewart,' said Bligh, 'we have outstayed our hospitality, I fear.'

'No, no,' cried Mr Stewart. 'The night is early. Stay, I beg you.'

'I regret any distress my foolish midshipman may have caused your daughter. It shall not happen again.'

'Never think of it,' said Mr Stewart. 'Women old and young are fickle creatures. Mr Brisco is in nowise to blame.'

'Concerning your ambitions for your son,' said Bligh, 'I regret that it is beyond my powers to do anything. I have no influence with their lordships of Admiralty.'

'You have honoured my house with your presence,' said Mr Stewart. 'I ask no more.'

'Goodnight, sir,' said Bligh to the darkling figure over by the window.

The young man made no answer. He did not so much as turn his head.

'Now,' said Lieutenant Bligh, 'are the water casks all secured? It is good water. I know that, I have been this way before. Pure spring water, out of a rock. We will leave with the first tide. Have you anything to report?'

Mr Andrews could hardly wait to unburden himself. If there was one thing he enjoyed on this ship, it was to play upon Bligh like a great double bass, to evoke growls and groans and gruffness at the recounting of some piece of indiscipline or folly.

'Eight seamen,' said Mr Andrews, 're-turned drunk from shore leave, in greater or lesser degrees of intoxication. I have noted their names, on this paper. They are...'

'Enough,' said Bligh. 'I do not want to hear their names. It was to be expected that a few of them would ring their coins on tavern counters. They were long enough at sea. Only eight? I expected more.'

'There is one serious case,' said Andrews. 'The seaman O'Rourke. He was not at the quayside, waiting, when his six hours were up. The boat lingered another half-hour. No O'Rourke. None of the sailors could tell us anything.'

'Well?'

'He was found, so drunk he could not

41

stand, in one of the lowest taverns in the village. He was being tended by some slut or doxy. Mr Brax says, if the dirt had been removed from her face, and a decent dress put on her, she might have been comely. When Brax and the two sailors heaved O'Rourke to his feet, she clung on to him, and asked, in the dreadful accent they have, what would become of him? One of the sailors loosed her hands from O'Rourke's shoulder. Mr Brax said it might prove a flogging matter, a dozen lashes. And at that she set up a terrible wailing. And they dragged O'Rourke backwards, his heels making furrows in the dust, all the way down to the longboat.'

'I see,' said Bligh.

'Will I have O'Rourke brought up for sentence?' said Mr Andrews.

'When one of my own officers can't control himself with liquor and females, what are we to expect of a common seaman? Let O'Rourke sleep off his foolishness. He will be ill and wretched when he wakens. That will be sufficient punishment.'

'There is one piece of good news, sir. I have found a carpenter, and a good one.'

'Well done, Mr Andrews.'

'A young man, sir, a year out of his apprenticeship. The name, Peter Linklater. I happened to stroll through the village in the evening, and there, in a yard above one of the little stone piers, a few men and boys were making fishing-boats, the kind with six oars. There were three, in various stages of construction. They are shy folk, those islanders. As soon as they saw me, they stopped speaking and turned their backs on me and concentrated on their hammering and sawing. "Now, lads," said I, "which of you has a venture—some spirit? Is there not one among you who longs to see the great places of earth, from the Americas to New Holland and every place between? That ship out there, she lacks a good carpenter..." Upon that they fell to their hammering and planing more eagerly than before. All but one young fellow, who turned a bright face on me, and smiled, and nodded, and took a few paces towards me. The oldest man there—he had a silver-flecked beard—cries out, "Peter, are you out of your mind! Peter, I've been a father to you! Peter, do you not know what life is like on those hell-ships?..." Then he turned to me. "Sir," said he, "this man Peter Linklater is my best workman. There is not his like in Orkney for handling and shaping of wood. Take Peter Linklater with you, and this poor boatyard of mine is finished..." "Peter," said I, "have your chest and belongings on board ship as soon as you can. We leave with tomorrow's tide..." We went up the steps together to the village street, Peter Linklater and I. The old man was crying after us: "Have I not lodged you and kept you since your mother died five winters ago in Shetland? You broke a hammer six weeks ago. You'll pay for that, my lad. What am I to tell Bella-Ann, that lass? O Peter, Peter, you'll wish a thousand times to be home again..." Peter, though I saw he had a certain remorse about deserting his master and workyard, stepped out with me resolutely enough. I gathered, from a few words he let fall, that all was not well between him and his Bella-Ann. And this is the principal reason for his wanting to leave Hamnavoe.'

'I don't want a wood-chopper aboard,' said Bligh. 'I don't want some silly handless fellow.'

'I think I can vouch for him, sir,' said Mr Andrews. 'The way he let his hand move over the wood of the ship. The light in his eyes when he saw our tools and workbench and the baulks of timber! He will be a treasure to the ship.'

'Yet I do not like his way of betraying his old master. If he did it once, a pattern is set—he may do it again.'

'I can vouch for him, sir. He will be loyal. It is a bruised heart he takes away from this place.'

'Women,' said Bligh. 'Always women. Where is the carpenter now?'

'He is to carry his box on board,' said Mr Andrews. 'He is ashore making last arrangements—settling up with the master boat-builder, making his adieux to Bella-Ann, having a last drink with his friends. He will be at the quay at noon.'

'I am glad of it,' said Bligh. 'Would you tell Brisco that I will see him now?'

'Sit down at the desk, man. You're as white in the face as a goose. You have a poor head for liquor. I want you to write out a letter for me. "To Alexander Stewart, esquire, at the White House, Hamnavoe.

"Sir, I thank you for your hospitality to me on the evening of yesterday. Convey my greetings to Mistress Stewart and to your family.

"I would return your hospitality, but my necessary business in your port is now completed, and *Resolution* sails with the tide at 2 o'clock this afternoon.

"With regard to a matter about which we had some words last night, viz., the possibility of your son's enlisting as a midshipman in His Majesty's Navy, I have, as I think I told you, no direct influence in matters of this kind. But I do know where suggestions may be made, and hints dropped, that may lead to the opening of doors.

"I have had long experience of dealing with men, especially men who feel themselves called to the sea.

"I observed your son closely, last night. Whatever words I may have said in your house, due to the stress of circumstances, I did form a most favourable impression of your son's character and calling, and I do not doubt that, if he gained entry into the service, he would acquit himself honourably and faithfully.

"I am in a short time to give up my command of this ship *Resolution*, having been called to other duties. There is a plan presently mooted—I put it no higher—of an expedition to the isles of Otaheite in the Pacific Ocean; which, should it come to pass, I have fair hopes of the command. The vessel, I am informed, may bear the fortunate name of *Bounty*.

"I have every hope of getting together a loyal crew for this enterprise, which will be devoted in the main to a certain experiment in that branch of science called botany. Should it succeed, it may prove of value in certain parts of the globe, as far as the bodily nourishment of the inhabitants is concerned; and this quite apart from any trading facilities that may have advantage to our nation.

"The venture will have certain difficulties and hazards. I need to be assured of the competence and loyalty of the men under my command.

"I now request you to inform George Stewart, your son, to hold himself in readiness, should he be willing to accompany me on this voyage. I will get word to you as soon as may be, by the usual post, or by some officer known to me who will have occasion to water at Hamnavoe. I do not doubt that the tidings will be good.

"Sir, I would ask you a favour. I am to sign on as ship's carpenter a young local man, by name Peter Linklater. I enclose three sovereigns with this letter. You would oblige me much by giving the enclosed coins to a certain young local woman of the name of Bella-Ann—I do not know her surname. And tell her, as from me, that Peter will be looked after, and may in the course of time return to her well seasoned and shaped by the hardships, the beauty and the mystery of the sea. The heart of a man, if it is true, returns none the worse for a far-faring.

"I think I apologised to you last night for the conduct of my midshipman..." '

'Must I put this down?' cried James Brisco from the desk, in a small agony of mortification.

'You will put down, sir, exactly what I

47

tell you to put down. Be glad that there are so few thorns in it—such as, that I will not recommend such as you to sail with me on the *Bounty*. If your hand is shaking, sir, it is because of the amount of drink you put down your throat last night. Are you ready? Take up the quill. Write "...for the conduct of my midshipman James Brisco, who availed himself too well and too foolishly of the ardent spirits on your sideboard, and so caused a measure of distress to your charming and talented daughter. Mr Brisco is to carry this letter to your house in person. I hope that, in person also, he will apologise for his indiscretion.

"I have the honour to be, Sir, your respectful servant..."

'Give me the pen. I will sign the letter. You are to carry it at once up to the White House. See that it is delivered into Mr Stewart's hands. That poor wife of his might put it behind the clock—it might not be discovered for a twelve-month.'

A quarter of an hour later, Bligh saw through his glass James Brisco land from the small boat at the steps of the quay: the white rectangle with the red wax splotch on it in his hand.

There, at the end of the pier, stood a young man with a box on his shoulder; the new ship's carpenter, Peter Linklater.

Bligh tilted his glass at the White House. There was no movement there. The door was shut.

Then, suddenly, the door opened, and Elizabeth Stewart ran out, the collie dog making wild circles about her, and the wind took her long hair and flung it out bright behind her. The girl knelt down and, laughing, embraced the dog. Then girl and dog turned and ran towards the rigs of green corn on the side of the hill. Even the bread of the islanders, thought Lieutenant Bligh, must have a slight salt taste to it.

The Laird's Son

1

I have just settled into my townhouse in the Canongate, and am looking forward with much eagerness to the winter entertainments of the city: the balls, the plays and operas, the soirées and elegant suppers. There are friends half-known, and many new friends—I am persuaded—to make acquaintance with. Already I have glimpsed the faces and figures of young ladies that I would know more intimately.

Tomorrow is the last day of November. It being St Andrew's Night, I am invited to meet Lady Stockbridge at her house in the Lawnmarket.

Simison is proving a useful servant indeed. He has aired and pressed my best suit, and the silver buttons shine like stars.

2

At Lady Stockbridge's, all went well. There was above a score of guests, most of them sedate and elderly, and only a few of an age with myself, but one, Miss Arabella Maxwell, who responded with a winning charm to my civilities. I hope to be better acquainted with this most beautiful young lady. The truth is, by the end of the evening Miss Arabella had cast a kind of enchantment on me. It would otherwise have been a tedious evening. Upon my kissing her hand adieu, she said, smiling, that she would desire a closer acquaintance. I pray that means may be found for such a flowering.

Earlier, after a round of whist, she had told me that six or seven winters since, she had been introduced—at the age of twelve—to the poet Burns, and recalled still the dark fire in his eyes, and his forthright manly speech.

I slept little, for the picture of Miss Maxwell came and went all night, a sweet torment.

Simison was disturbed at my poor appetite next morning. 'You maun eat,' said he, 'or you'll dwine and die like that puir brither o' yours.'

3

Disturbing news from London this morning.

My father was taken ill in the Parliament last week, and is confined to his rooms. It seems it is some sort of heart seizure. His writing, so firm and elegant normally, is frail and wayward and broken on the page. Yet the sense is clear enough. 'It is ever my custom to spend the dark time of the year in my Hall in Shetland, as you know. There is much requiring attention, such as the report of Williamson the factor regarding the state of my holdings there, and whether the rents and other dues have been well accounted for, not to speak of the welfare of the tenants as regards their crofts and fishing-boats, and any disputes which may have arisen... Since I cannot sail north myself, and as death has so recently claimed my dear heir your brother, you will make all due haste to take ship from Leith into Shetland. Williamson will make plain to you those matters you might have difficulty with...'

4

Yesterday, with a heavy heart, I took leave of Miss Arabella in her mother's house at the Potter-row. She gave me many tokens of her regard. Had her mother not been present, I do not know how it would have gone with me, for after the tea drinking—it being then time to take farewell—the tremor in my heart rose up to my mouth—and I turned away to hide from them the sorrow o'erbrimming my eyes. And yet I hoped that the dear young lady had noticed the tears, and that they had been for her a sufficient indication of my affections.

Simison has arranged everything. He had spoken this morning in Leith with the skipper of the barque *Vesper;* they have agreed terms for a passage into Shetland.

5

I cannot adequately tell what utter misery I endured on that voyage. In the Moray Firth, and again betwixt Fair Isle and Sumburgh, such dreadful sea spasms afflicted me that I cared not if I died.

Added to those physical sufferings was the prospect of weeks spent among a half-savage peasantry, of whose language and customs I knew nothing; conning account books in some cold boreal office with Mr Williamson, a dull pedantic man, by all accounts.

When I thought of that dark place, at the very darkest stormiest part of the year, far from the social whirl of Edinburgh, and lacking in particular the radiancy and the ardour of Arabella, my heart turned to stone.

6

Mistress Williamson has made as comfortable as can be two rooms in the twenty-chambered Hall, and there I am to endure my exile. May it be brief!

I recovered quickly from my sea sickness.

I slept a full round of the clock; the sound of silver and china awakened me; I found the good woman arranging on a bedside table a dish of fish and eggs, butter and cheese and bannocks, all of which tasted delicious after that anguished enforced fast upon the baleful waters of the German Ocean.

The fire burned bright—I washed and dressed with care. The low sun at noon was but a handsbreadth over the southern horizon.

Against that light I saw a crew of fishermen coming up from the shore with baskets of fish, and their womenfolk came to meet them on the sea-banks above.

'Now,' thought I, 'if it so chances that my father dies, as he may do soon, as he will of a certainty do in the course of time, those people will be my people, together with the wretched hovels that they live in and likewise their fishing-boats and booths.'

I had small relish in the prospect.

The sun went down in mid-afternoon.

I walked among the scattered township of houses. The peasants who saw me coming turned their backs on me, or made haste to go indoors.

The darkling air was cold and quiet.

Mistress Williamson set before me a dinner of skate-fish and kale and potatoes, which I enjoyed more than I had anticipated.

Williamson came to my room. He neither knocked nor removed his bonnet. He said surlily that he would discuss the accounts, complaints, petitions with me in the morning.

'You will please to knock before you enter,' I said.

He glowered at me, and left.

I wrote by candlelight a long letter to Arabella; but put not my whole heart into it, being sure that the epistle would be over-read by her mother.

In the evening the Williamsons returned as always to their own house by the gate, and I was alone in the great house.

I answered a knock at the door.

There, framed in starlight, stood a young woman.

I could not understand a word of her

lingo, it being imbued (as I supposed) with Norwegian words and cadences.

I did comprehend that she came from the croft of Scad, and that her name was Betsy.

And she held out to me a fish: 'Da best o' da catch,' as a welcome offering.

7

I have brought in my chest Crabbe's *Poems* and *The Man of Feeling* to while away the dark days.

Williamson knocks on my door about noon. A grim and a louring visage. Would I come now to the office to oversee the account books? No 'please' or 'by your leave' or 'sir' for Williamson. Had the ripples of the late upheavals in France reached as far as Thule?

The ledger he opened on the desk, though clear enough as to the script, might have been Egyptian hieroglyphics, or Chinese runes. He pointed here and there, on this item and its accompanying figure, and explained the significance. This lasted for upwards of an hour, his finger moving down the columns, until my attention faltered and plummeted like a wounded moor-bird. 'Very good, Williamson,' I said. 'You have been a good steward. I will report to my father that all is well with his estate in Shetland.'

But the factor was not to be put off by false flattery nor ill-simulated comprehension.

'It is far from well,' he said gloomily. 'I would that your father were here to knock a few heads together. Not only are they behind-hand with their rents, some of them grossly this year, but they conceal their fish-landings so that the Hall never gets its due share. And furthermore I know well that twelve firkins of geneva spirits were set ashore here from the Dutch vessel in the dark of the moon in November, forby a cask of tobacco, and all hidden in caves known only to themselves. Forby, they distil illicit whisky here and there in the hills. Not only your father's estate is cheated of its due, but the king's exchequer is set at naught. And forby they are riddled through and through with dark popish superstitions, that old MacTavish up at the Manse is powerless to uproot, though he does his best, Sabbath after Sabbath, with long weighty discourses, the poor old man.'

I had not thought the factor to have so much passion in him.

The rage subsiding, he once more put his finger here and there on the accounts book, gloomily equating this with that, expenditure on boats and gear balanced against meagre catches; and shaking his head at the ingratitude and mulishness of the tenants.

From the rigmarole I raised my head and saw through the window the girl that had called on me with the gift of fish on the previous evening. She was going betwixt byre and croft with a wooden bucket, so brimming full that a little milk slurped from it over the flagstones with every step she took, and made white star-splashes.

Betsy set down the milk pail. She glanced up at the high Hall window. She shaded her eyes against the level sun and raised her free hand to greet me.

Williamson saw that my attention had strayed. 'You will have to be well acquainted with this ledger,' said he, 'and all the disproportions in it, if you are to make these people aware of their obligations. Your father—the good Lord preserve him—had to bring them to task winter after winter, sternly.'

Williamson bestowed on me a look of smouldering contempt and distrust. A great pity (he was thinking) that the dependable son had to die so untimely. This whelp understood nothing, and seemed incapable of learning.

'I will visit the crofts,' I said, 'if that is expected of me.'

'I will come with you,' said Williamson. 'We will confront them, household by household, for the next week. We will make a few faces blanch.'

I made no reply. It seemed to me that I might get a better guide.

8

There is only a small segment of daylight now, at midwinter, in an immense star-thronged wheel of darkness.

I breakfasted at dawn. The wind began to blow from the west, and increased, until the timbers of the Hall creaked and groaned.

I put on coat and hat, and took my cane, and set my head into the gale, walking along the high cliffs, buffeted this way and that. I saw on a beach two groups of fishermen. They debated with themselves for a while, then stowed their gear in the bothies and turned for home, it seemed reluctantly.

'Indeed no one could fish in such seas,' I thought. The ocean was throwing great bell-beating waves high up the shore, and bursting in flurries of spume against the crags.

As I struggled with the wind, a kind of joy took possession of me that I hadn't known before in all my life. I found myself thinking, 'Rather this than drinking claret in Glencairns' in the Canongate—better this rage in the air than laying out cards for whist in Lady Stockbridge's drawing room.'

I almost thought, 'This is better than listening to Arabella Maxwell playing on the clavichord in Potter-row', but I quenched that ungallantry at its source.

And there, on a further beach, I saw the girl Betsy. She was helping three men to unload caisies of fish from a yole.

How could such a frail craft have lived through this tempest?

The men stowed their gear in the black-tarred hut.

Betsy lingered.

The men walked up the steep path to the road above, carrying the baskets of fish.

I said to the girl, 'I thought that fishing would be all but impossible in weather like this.'

'There's your rent to pay,' said Betsy, 'and Yule's nearly on us, and no fishing will be done from Tammasmas on.'

'I have to visit all the crofts in the township,' I said. 'My father has bidden me have a care and a keeping of his people. But I do not know either the crofts or the tenants.'

'I will show you,' said the girl.

In the little cluster of cottages along the shore I was received with grave courtesy.

Betsy went in at each door and introduced me to the crofter and his wife and children.

In one croft there were many children, six or seven; the tumult and cries were gathered to silence out of respect for the stranger.

In another, there was a solitary old man. His wife had died thirty years since. His three sons had been drowned not long after when the fishing-boat had been overset.

I think I have not known such courtesy in any gentleman's house, the length and breadth of the land.

In another house, a young wife was raging at her man for a wastrel and a drunkard. Hadn't he been three days in Scalloway with the sheep to sell, and come home blear-eyed and penniless! And what would the bairns do for coats in the snow? Then Betsy led me into the lamplight; at once the young wife hastened to put a plate of oatcakes and a flagon of whisky on the table for me. The children slept through the rage and the silence.

In two or three of the cottages, there

were old folk—the grandfathers and grand-mothers—sitting at the fire, and I saw what natural respect was accorded them, and how their words were listened to like a distillation of the wisdom of generations (I could not help thinking of certain young educated high-born sons who would watch their fathers like hawks for signs of mortality, and of their own enlargement and affluence).

In a certain poor house—two middle-aged brothers lived in it and a pale mute sister—one of the brothers, after the civil introduction, turned on me and said coldly that the lairds had done ill by the people, and had waxed rich over many generations on the hard labour of the islanders on land and sea. 'And now look at us,' said he, 'not fit for work, dependent on the good folk round about for bread and milk and fish...'

All this Betsy interpreted for me; for his speech was so richly Nordic that I only comprehended a word here and there... 'And yet,' said this rural Jacobin when his indignation had guttered out, 'may peace be with thee.'

Betsy explained to me that the brothers had both been press-ganged from a coastal cargo-vessel into the navy, and come home discharged after a decade to find the well-kept croft fallen to decay on account of the sister's lingering decline.

In one croft, the old man let go of my hand and took down a fiddle from the wall and struck out the native music with such gusto that the hens fluttered and squawked in the rafters above and the collie, barked and a pig grunted at the dark side of the fire wall, and his daughter cried, 'Enough, Lowrie, enough! Mr Stamford hasna come a' the wey f'ae Embro to listen to thee wild scratchings and scrapings!' And then, once more, the offering of a cup of rum and oat-cakes.

Betsy said, as we left for yet another house, 'Yon was the best welcome old Lowrie could pay thee.'

We crossed a field to another house set under a little green hill...

10

These visitations, so novel and delightful to me—the delight enhanced by the presence, day after day, of my winsome forthright guide—were but the groundwork and the prelude to a pure mysterious ritual that went on for many days and nights. I could not have comprehended this midwinter ceremony had not Betsy been there to explain all.

I saw how crosses made of straw had

already been affixed to the lintels of barn and byre. This, said the girl, was to protect the animals from the trows, malignant chthonic misshapen creatures that roamed the countryside in great hordes by night to put sickness on the winter-fast animals.

And the evil creatures that dwelt inside the hills and the knolls could come into the dwellings when all the good folk were asleep and steal the children out of the cradles, and leave behind their own deformed and sickly offspring. But the straw crosses kept them away.

On the night of December the twentieth, I was privileged to witness the ceremony for the protection of children.

A very old woman—the grandmother—in the house of the many children, bent with a candle over the various cribs, chanting in a low solemn voice:

Mary Midder, haad de hand
Ower aboot for sleeping-band,
Haad da lass and haad da wife,
Haad da bairn a' its life.
Mary Midder, haad de hand
Roond da infants o' oor land.

The next day was Thomasmas, December the twenty-first.

It was, I noticed, a calm luminous day on the sea, 'as good a day for

64

fishing as we're like to see this winter,' Williamson said.

But not one boat put out with lines and bait.

I visited Betsy's father and two brothers who sat smoking their pipes on a bench at the end of their house. They said nothing. They turned away from me. I think they are a little put out that their lass is so familiar with the son of the Hall. There is something, they consider, not right about that, something clean contrary to the social order. Betsy ought to know better.

At sunset on the shortest day Betsy spoke the rhyme that prohibits all work whatsoever on Thomasmas Day:

The very babe unborn
Cries 'O dule! dule!'
For the breaking o' Tammasmas Night
Five nights afore Yule.

Three nights later, on Christmas Eve, I saw the old fiddler beside his barn lifting the upper quernstone from the lower stone and, slowly and solemnly, taking it inside.

Then, crofter by crofter, the same piece of ritual was enacted: the stone that turned and ground the bread lifted and removed to a safe place.

'For why?' said Betsy. 'For this is the

night that the trows come and turn the quern wheel against the sun. And if that happens, the stones will be barren, there'll be no meal and bread next harvest, the countryside'll starve. And your father won't get a penny in rent...'

That same night Betsy took me to the house of the scolding wife and the man who had sold the sheep for drink in Scalloway. He did not behave like a wastrel in the little lamp-splashed room; he seemed like a celebrant in some ancient mystery.

The wife brought out a basin and filled it with water. The man lifted three live embers from the fire and dropped them one by one from the tongs into the water, with small hissings and wisps of steam. Then he washed his hands and face in the singed water. His wife went through the same lustration. The three children dipped hands and faces and lifted them, streaming... Across the bed were laid out the clean clothes that every member of the family would wear on Christmas morning.

'And now,' said Betsy, 'I must hurry home. The same thing's to be done there, and in every other house in Shetland... Be sure to be here in the morning, before sunrise.'

In the late lingering twilight of Yule

morning I stood at a corner of the barn of Scad. Betsy's father came out of the cottage, guided by a flickering candle in a stark shadowy holder; and he went slowly into the byre where the cow and the ox were stalled. I came quietly and stood in the open door, watching. Old Ollie seemed unaware of my presence. I saw, startled, that the candleholder was a cow's skull. Ollie spoke familiarly to the beasts, but in the old tongue I could not understand him, and the beasts mingled their lowings with his chant. I think he must have been telling them that Christ was born—now they had nothing to fear—the powers of evil could not touch any living creature on such a marvellous morning. The light flowering out of the skull was an extraordinary symbol. I stood there, deeply moved.

Then the old man forked hay into the stall recklessly, and the beasts munched at their breakfast, astonished at its abundance; for in the depths of winter their provender is of necessity meagre, the store of hay having to last till new grasses of spring are on the hillside.

Ollie seemed to bless the animals with his hand. When he blew out the candle the dawn light was coming in at the byre door, and his face shone.

I left the steading quickly, as if I had intruded on some blessed place.

I saw that now every window in the township was lit. A spy and an intruder still, I went and stood at the small window of Steethe, the house of the many children. The table was set for a festive meal—not the coarse oat bannocks and thin ale of an ordinary breakfast, but at every place round the board there had been set a yellow cake, each with a flared edge so that it seemed to represent the sun. One by one, from the eldest to the youngest, the children lit candles at the hearth-flame, and set the small chaste flames here and there about the house, in the wall-niches and on the meal-chest, on table and hearthstone and over the bed and the door lintel, till the interior was steeped in most lovely light. Each one of the family wore the clean clothes that had been set out the previous night, and their earth-grained faces shone from the lustral washing.

Meantime the man of the house had filled a little wooden keg from a stone jar of whisky. He drank from it himself, then presented the vessel to his wife, who after sipping had much ado to force the fierce sun-essence down. Then the father went round the table, in a solemn sunward circle, and he touched a drop of the spirit to the lips of each child. Then he sat at the high table and broke his own sun-cake and put the pieces into his mouth: in token of ripeness and abundance, light and warmth.

11

The Williamsons do not celebrate Christmas; Mrs Williamson brought up to my room the usual plate of eggs and barley-scones and a jug of tea.

The factor was standing at the office door when I came down, ready for business.

'A good Yule to you,' I said.

'Good morning,' he said. 'There are letters, one I think in your father's hand. They arrived on the *Swedish Lass* yesterday, from Lerwick. But you were not here to receive them. I hear you have been busy these past days making closer acquaintance with your future tenants. I trust you have been enlightened.'

The letter from my father was in his wonted firm hand. 'I am quite recovered from my indisposition, but I am advised to go to some resort, probably Bath, to take the waters there. I am sure you have learned much from Williamson, who has always been a good honest faithful servant to me. And furthermore you will now have experience of the land and the fishing and of the intricacies of our rent systems and of the deviousness and obstinacy of the folk you will have the care and keeping and ordering of when I am no longer here. Doubtless you will be missing the social delights of Edinburgh, and will take the opportunity of the first south-bound passage out of Shetland. Do whatever your impulses dictate, and may it fare well with you...'

The second letter was from Mrs Maxwell of the Potter-row in Edinburgh. 'My daughter Arabella, I am happy to inform you, was upon the ninth inst. betrothed to Lieutenant MacAulay of the Scots Guards. In these times of war, it is as yet uncertain when the marriage can take place. Lieutenant MacAulay has been ordered to rejoin his regiment before the end of the year. I trust you are benefiting much by your stay in your family estate in the Shetlands. Pray do us the honour of calling upon your return, whenever that may be.'

A week ago, that letter would have stabbed me to the heart.

The truth is, I have hardly given Arabella a thought since the night that Betsy stood at the Hall door with a gift of fish for me.

I told Williamson that my father seemed now fully recovered. For the first time, I saw the man smile. He was not to

70

be lumbered with a bookish ineffectual liberal-minded laird, at least not for the present.

To overbrim his joy, I set a guinea on the desk beside ledger and inkpot and quills. 'A Yule gift,' I said.

The shadow set on his brows again. 'Let it lie,' he said, 'till the fires of their superstition die down.'

He did not thank me. He left the golden coin to gather dust there until Twelfth Night was over, and the world was grey and earnest once more.

12

Betsy told me that I ought to stay till Up-Helly-Aa, when the young men drag a barrel blazing with tar through the township, some time in January.

This, I take it, signals the final triumph of the sun after the winter darkness, flame answering flame.

'It's a grand time, Up-Helly-Aa,' said Betsy.

Williamson brought word that same afternoon that the brig *Loudon* was in Lerwick, and would embark for Aberdeen, Leith, Newcastle and Gravesend with a cargo of salted fish and kelp two days hence.

Why was my heart so heavy, as Williamson's horse-and-trap lurched along the broken road to Lerwick and the brig *Loudon?* There were no crofters to wave me a farewell at the end of the road.

The carriage swayed round a corner, and there was a young woman driving three ewes across the hill, in the first swirlings of winter snow.

Betsy raised her hand, a farewell and a pledge. Perhaps a kiss trembled in the darkening air between us.

The Children's Feast

There were twelve shops along the street of the small town: the butcher, the baker, the shoemaker, the confectioner, the grocer, the tobacconist, the draper, the fish-shop, and Mr Rousay the general merchant. (A few others were kept by old wives who sold sweeties and odds and ends.) The general merchant's was the really big shop—an emporium—and Mr Rousay sold everything—drapery, fish and flesh, needles and anchors, sweet-stuffs and groceries, knitted goods, magazines and books, ironmongery: *everything*.

In this small town by the sea, Christmas —or Yule as most folk called it—had not for a very long time been kept as a holiday. Instead, they had a wild whirl of whisky, fiddles and dancing for three days round about New Year, a week later.

It may have been the influence of a new stratum of society in the islands, the professional class (teachers, doctors, lawyers, shipping agents, excisemen) that put Yuletide in a new favourable light. At any rate, the provost, magistrates and councillors at their monthly meeting in November decided that 25 December would be a holiday, and all places of business would be closed.

Not everybody was pleased. Some of the shopkeepers said it would be bad for business—they had little enough profit as it was. The man most outspoken against this Yule holiday was Timothy Rousay, the general merchant, an elder and councillor and justice of the peace. He was reputed to be the very richest man in the town, with upwards of a thousand pounds in the bank. He it was, of all the councillors, who had moved in council against this newfangled idle day in midwinter. And a few kirk elders muttered that popish practices were beginning to impinge. And some townsfolk said it was the English newspapers in the public library that were filling the folks' minds with all kinds of newfangled nonsense.

But in general it was agreed that they would observe the Yule holiday—for this one year anyway, to see how it went. (In the days of their grandfathers it had been a wonderful week-long festival.)

It must be said that this particular year had been a very bad winter in Orkney, almost the worst that anyone could remember. There was deep poverty in the crofts and along the fishing piers. An appeal had been sent to Edinburgh for relief supplies to be sent north; but so far no answer had come, no deep-cargoed ship had been sighted off Hoy.

It was said that, that winter, the tinkers were better off than the smaller crofters. Being closer in touch with the sources of existence, it seemed those vagrants could wring nourishment out of stones and roots.

As for the children—when Mr Tellford the schoolmaster told them on 24 December that next day would be a holiday from school, there was in the playground an outburst of joy. A few first flakes of snow were beginning to drift down out of the early darkness. The scholars danced and cheered as if the snowflakes were a bounty of shillings and crowns. Their boots rang on the frosty cobbles.

Later the bellman walked through the street announcing at every station along the way: 'Tomorrow will be observed as a holiday in the burgh, and all shops and offices will be closed, by order of the council...'

Some children followed the joyous clang of the bell and the sonorous proclamation of Peter Spence the bellman all along the street. When the bellman folded his bell at the far end of the village (the last bronze echo dying away) and went into the alehouse to soothe his throat after all that outcry, there was nothing left for the kids to do but press their cold faces against the shop windows, with treasures inside of apples, chocolate, boiled sweets, cinnamon biscuits, cheese, sausages, black liquorice sticks...

The snow fell thicker about them. The sky was dark and there was not a star to be seen.

In one shop window a single candle glowed and dribbled in an old wine bottle. There was nothing on display, nothing at all, not so much as a fishbone or a mouldy crust. The window was empty.

But the children saw the old general merchant, Timothy Rousay, sitting at his desk inside, going through his ledger, page after page of bad debts, with a blunt pencil; sometimes scowling, sometimes smirking; often pausing to make a mark on the glimmering page.

'This beats all,' said Moll Spence at the close-end to Jemima Stevenson. 'All the shops are closed, all the offices, the six pubs and the school and the post office and the bank too. But the old skinflint is open for business as usual.'

The winged word went from end to end of the village. It was Christmas morning, and the village though deep in snow

76

was tranced and dazzled with light, for the morning sun came flashing from the still blue harbour water and the unsullied celestial blueness.

The housewives stood round the well with their pails, pitchers, buckets, and shook their heads. 'A miser—what greed!...' 'It'll do him no good, the old sinner...' 'There's no pockets in shrouds...' 'Not a soul to leave it to, all his guineas and sovereigns...' 'Oh yes he's tempting Providence, the greedy wretch...' 'He'd scratch hell for a ha'penny, that man.'

So the chorus of women stood in a circle and with one voice they passed judgement on the richest man in Hamnavoe, Timothy Rousay.

A boy ran past along the street, and the scoop of his jersey that he held out with both hands was weighted to overflowing with oranges, apples and bananas.

A girl ran past with a straw basket on her arm; and the Hamnavoe housewives knew pots of syrup and jams, and packets of sugar and tea, when they saw them.

They had not time to wonder where the parents of those bairns—fishing folk—had the money to buy such delicacies, in this the poorest winter in folks' minding, when the widow's boy Pat Fara came stumbling through the snow carrying in front of him on a big plate a pig's head, with an orange in its gob.

And after Pat Fara came Johnny Cauldhame staggering under a sack of coal, and there was a Jamaica rum flask sticking out of his jacket pocket. (It was known that Johnny Cauldhame's father was bad with bronchitis, and had not been able to cut and cart peats in the summer.)

Then, a few seconds later, a boy came as if he was wearing armour, he clanged so much. Bert Kerston, challenged by the women on his homeward trudge through the snow, opened his sack and showed them a hoard of tins and cans: salmon, corned beef, rice and pears and peaches and pineapples, beans and beetroot—all this foreign stuff that, it was said, would last forever, locked in metal. Bert Kerston took a tin-opener from his pocket and went on, laughing, to his hungry house at the end of the pier.

The women, in a wondering silence, wound their dripping buckets up from the well in the middle of the town. (And it was not often that these chatterers and keeners and legend-bearers were ever reduced to silence: the last time had been when Queen Victoria's son Alfred, Duke of Edinburgh, had walked through the street to the Town Hall—a royal prince in their midst! That had hushed their mouths like flowers for an hour till Prince Alfred in his admiral's uniform had gone aboard his launch below the Town Hall.)

The tinkers had been in their tents since early December, in the quarry at the far end of the town, and they had no money and only miscellaneous rags to keep out the bitter weather. No one wanted to buy their tin pots and spoons this winter. While the women of Hamnavoe wound up their pails of water, one after another, in a trance of silence—and each face momentarily transfigured when the sun came flashing off the trembling water surfaces—by came the tinker twins Toby and Tess, and they were laden like far-travelled merchants with coats, scarves, stockings, gloves, shawls and bonnets; and on past the well they went with their burdens of warmth as though they were bound on an expedition to Spitzbergen.

Along came Peter Spence the bellman, glum and mutinous because all the six pubs were closed. 'A disgrace,' he said. 'I'll write to the Member of Parliament... And all this snow. And not a drop of whisky to be had! The frost could grip a man's heart—I've heard of such a thing.'

'And why,' said Moll Spence to him sweetly, 'why, Peter man, don't you go along to Tim Rousay's shop? He's giving away things for nothing this morning.

You'd get a bottle of Old Orkney malt, for sure.'

'Haven't I tried?' said the bellman. 'I pleaded with him. I offered him three shillings for a bottle, instead of the usual half-a-crown... And do you know what he said, the skinflint? "Peter," says he, "only the bairns are getting served today".'

And Peter passed on, to try his luck at the back door of Maggie Marwick's, who kept The White Horse at the end of the village.

After that, Christmas was always observed in Hamnavoe, though the pristine purity was increasingly dulled by such things as greetings cards, decorations, paper bells, plum puddings and mince pies.

Next Christmas Timothy Rousay, councillor, kirk elder, justice of the peace—was lying in the kirkyard, and as yet no one has thought to put up a gravestone to him.

When the lawyer and the banker went through his ledger, after the funeral, they discovered that he was not a rich man at all.

He had warmed his thin blue hands at that one fire, and the children of Hamnavoe had danced round about it; and then he had said 'Goodnight' to the world and closed his door for the last time.

A Crusader's Christmas

1

It had been a bad storm: such rages of wind and sea from the east, that the fifteen pilgrim ships from Norway and Orkney at the end of summer had been driven back from southern France towards the coast of Spain.

In Narbonne in southern France the crusaders had lingered all that autumn. The leader of the expedition, Earl Rognvald Kolson of Orkney, had fallen in love with the Countess of Narbonne, Ermengarde. His harp brimmed with lyric after lyric.

Golden one,
Tall one
Moving in perfume and onyx,
Witty one,
You with the shoulders
Lapped in long silken hair,
Listen: because of me
The eagle has a red claw.

The sailors—Norwegians and Icelanders and Orkneymen—had not objected to the long sojourn in Narbonne. The wine casks in the taverns and the black-haired French girls: coming from their cold northern bourne, they had not imagined such delights.

The old Bishop of Orkney, William, kept reminding them that they were engaged on a special voyage, a penitential pilgrimage to the holy eastern places, so that they might wash off their hands the old encrustings of Viking murder and pillage.

The sailors answered: they were there to obey the commands of their captain, Earl Rognvald.

At last, in mid-December, the earl managed to tear himself from the honied web in which he had let himself be entangled.

The lady Ermengarde looked through her window one morning to see the fifteen Scandinavian ships drifting one after another out of the harbour.

2

Out in the Mediterranean, the easterly gale struck them suddenly. The ships staggered. Drenches of sea fell inboard and not only dispirited the crews—made soft with months of Provençal luxury—but ruined their stores of food and water.

'Nothing for it,' cried the cold sailors, 'we must go back to Narbonne...' And the thought of that cheered them in their misery.

Bishop William said, 'We will never go back to Narbonne.' Earl Rognvald ordered the fleet to put about and seek shelter in a Spanish harbour.

3

The Spanish port—the sagamen haven't given it a name; let's call it San Juan—had an ample harbour.

San Juan had sent down a delegation to meet the Norse captains as they rowed ashore. But there were no welcoming hands or speeches.

Earl Rognvald explained to the mayor how things stood with the fleet: stores ruined, water-barrels staved in. He would be glad to buy as many provisions as the countryside could provide: beef, pork, geese, cheeses, eggs, oranges, olives, wine casks.

The earl's treasurer unthonged a money-bag and poured out a stream of gold and silver coins into his free palm.

The merchants' eyes shone with greed.

But the mayor shook his head. There would be no deal. He pointed to a large fortified house that stood among the foothills a mile away. He shook his fist at the keep and stamped his foot. His head trembled with anger.

Neither the earl nor the bishop nor the captains could find a meaning to this bitter mime.

At last it came out. The castellan and his soldiers battened on the village. They had sucked the village dry for a year and more. If the people of San Juan objected to those arbitrary 'taxes', the men in the castle dealt out bloody noses and broken bones. In the darkness of night a villager would waken to find his roof burning. The village women were molested whenever they strayed beyond the gate of the olive grove.

'I'll be blunt with you,' said Sebastian the mayor to Earl Rognvald. 'You could do us a good turn by destroying that castle. We're not exactly green hereabouts. We have abundance of food and wine stored, where those beasts from the castle will never find them. If you ice-men from the north break the castle, break it and burn it and spread the stones of it a mile wide, you can have provisions that will lade your ships to the gunwale... If not, just leave us in peace. We have enough on our hands with the taxmen and the soldiers from the castle. The name of the castellan, by the way, is Godfrey. Watch him, he's cunning and slippery as a snake.'

Earl Rognvald consulted with the captains. Some of them were in favour of attacking the castle; like their ancestors, they had a relish for such danger and possible rich rewards. Others were for sacking the village and finding the hidden stores and stocking the fifteen ships and celebrating Yule at sea with sirloins and horns of sweet Spanish wine.

The bishop had gone back to his own ship to read his Advent psalms.

Earl Rognvald told the captains that they would attack the castle as soon as the battering-rams and the ladders were ready—as soon as the rusty swords and axes had been scoured, and the bows strung and the arrows tipped with iron. Let the men be told.

4

The Norse sailors swarmed out of the ships that same day, a great host.

They were hungry and cold.

They looked, in the late afternoon, at the lamps burning in the windows of the castle, and the watchfires on the battlements.

Yes, they assured the earl, they liked the idea of an assault at dawn the next day.

Sebastian and the people of San Juan had taken the precaution of shuttering their windows and barring their doors. Northern ships were not to be trusted.

The wind blew from the castle enchanting smells of roasted beef and new-baked bread.

The Norsemen returned hungry to the ships to put keen edges on their weapons.

The pilgrim-crusaders woke. The sun shone. The golden figurehead on Earl Rognvald's ship glittered with dawn and winter frost.

The bishop chanted from his ship: 'Lift up your gates, O ye princes...'

5

Before noon the Norse host was drawn up in ranks under the castle, just out of arrow-range.

A man in a rich tapestried coat came and stood on the castle battlement. He made a trumpet of his hands and hailed the besiegers. 'Welcome to Spain, Earl Rognvald Kolson and you other captains out of the north. We would be pleased if you spent Christmas here with us in the castle. You look as if you could do with some roasted goose and old wine. It is cold at sea at this time of year. In the castle we have good fires going night and day, and music and poetry. Our women are thought to be beautiful enough. We will open the gates for you. Only, I would consider it a favour if you returned your axes and swords and daggers and arrows to the ships.'

Godfrey the castellan had a deep rich cultured voice, quite other than the surly ungraciousness of Sebastian and the villagers of San Juan.

There was a young Norwegian captain called Eindred. Eindred urged the earl to accept Godfrey's hospitality.

It should be said that those sailor-pilgrims from the north were not a united host.

Right from the start of the voyage Eindred had been a trouble to the earl. When the fleet was being built in Norwegian shipyards, Eindred had encrusted part of his ship with gold—poop and figurehead and weathercocks—whereas it had been agreed beforehand that only Rognvald's ship was to have such embellishment. All down the North Sea and into Biscay, Eindred had striven to sail in the van of the fleet—an insult to the commander-in-chief.

Earl Rognvald stood now in front of the host: 'Get ready to attack the castle.'

The men raised a great shout. The castle battlement was lined with people: cooks and ostlers and sempstresses.

The villagers of San Juan opened their shutters and stuck out their heads like gargoyles.

The first arrow flew from a Norse bow towards the castle.

A man in a mitre and crozier walked up from the shore: Bishop William with the silver beard.

'I shouldn't have to tell you, Rognvald Kolson, that today is Nativity Eve. The Prince of Peace will be born on earth this very night. There will be no fighting from now till Twelfth Night. See to it.'

Earl Rognvald ordered the men to return to the ships.

Eindred curled his lip in contempt and mockery.

Up on the castle battlement, Godfrey laughed.

Sebastian and the village men nodded, and closed the shutters.

That day, on shipboard, the sailors ate salt fish for their dinner and drank French wine that had gone sour.

6

In the village of San Juan, at midnight, the priest said the Mass of the Nativity: 'The Lord hath said to me, Thou art My Son, this day have I begotten Thee...'

Earl Rognvald saw, kneeling not far from him, Godfrey the castellan, and Sebastian the mayor on the other side.

The little church was crowded with fishermen and peasants and their women. All knelt. They were adrift on silence and candlelight.

A small bell rang.

Christ had come upon earth, among the animals, angels, shepherds, kings.

The worshippers were pierced by a star of wonderment.

7

All the twelve hungry days between Yule and Epiphany, the Norse crews bivouacked in the fields between the village and the castle.

At night the sailors lit great fires. Over the flames they cooked fish and hares and birds: whatever they had managed to catch that day.

They drank water from a little stream that ran down, cold and green, from the mountains.

Eindred and the Norwegians sat at a different fire from the Orkneymen and the Icelanders.

A beggarman wandered into the camp. Eindred invited the man to sit at his fire, and shared a morsel of fish with him. The young Norwegian aristocrat and the old Spanish beggar whispered together for a long time under the stars.

At last the beggar got to his feet and walked off into the darkness.

'Now,' said Earl Rognvald to Thorbjorn Black the poet, 'that man, under his rags and filth, looks to me very like our friend Godfrey from the castle.'

8

On the morning following Twelfth Night, the Norse warmen attacked the castle.

Eindred asked, as a particular favour, that he might attack from the north. But once the assault was under way, it was noticed that there was little activity in Eindred's host.

The first assault was a failure. The ladders were thrown down. Burning pitch was poured on the men who were trying to smash open the locks of the bronze-studded oak doors with their axes. From the high battlements the castle archers picked off man after man in the seething ranks behind.

'Valhalla will be boisterous with heroes tonight,' said the poet Arnor, licking blood from his wrist that a Spanish arrow had grazed.

There was still no movement from Eindred's host stationed to the north of the castle.

From time to time Godfrey appeared on a battlement, and gravely saluted the earl.

'Earl Rognvald,' he shouted in a lull of the fighting, 'you are a man of authority like me. You should understand how things stand here, in this part of Spain. Here in the castle we keep the lawbook, the swords of civil peace, the harps and the scrolls of verse on fine vellum. If it were not for my horsemen and my swords, all this coast and countryside would be anarchy and bloodshed. There are bandits in the mountains. Only the castle stands between the village and those lawless murderers in the caves up there. Of course we have to tax the villagers twice a year, roughly a tenth of the produce of their vineyards, olive groves, fishing grounds. It is for their own good and protection. Do you do less in your own Orkney earldom? How else do you keep your people from the longships of the Vikings?'

Earl Rognvald had nothing to say to that.

One of the captains, a shrewd man called Einar Ormson, took Earl Rognvald aside and said, 'I've noticed that the walls of the castle are poorly cemented. We've made five assaults and each time we've been driven back. We can't afford to lose more sailors. There's only one way to get into that castle, and that is to pile kindling all round the base and soak it in oil and fat and put the torches to it. I don't think the stonework could endure such fires.'

At once preparations for the conflagration were set in motion. The villagers came with anything that could be burnt: logs and tar barrels, goose fat and swine fat, old cribs and thwarts and oars with woodworm in them, nets and thatch, and over all they poured old rancid oil from cob-webbed jars in their cellars. Then the torches were thrust in, and the castle walls were lapped in flame.

The wind off the sea made the fires roar and rampage.

Stones began to fall from the castle walls here and there.

From the courtyard inside rose a lamentation of women.

The smoke of the burning rolled away

92

north, so that Eindred and his immobile army looked like ghosts.

Suddenly, from end to end a great fissure tore one wall of the castle apart. A battlement collapsed. Stones came thundering down, hot and reeking.

'Bring water,' cried Einar.

The villagers nearly fell over themselves, bringing up buckets of water from the well—a long chain of splashing wooden buckets—that the Norse warriors poured over the hot stones.

Steam rose from the broken walls and mingled with the smoke. Now Eindred and his men were lost in that thick fog.

The Norsemen poured into the breach.

Earl Rognvald gave leave for the peaceful people in the castle to depart. Out they trooped, white-faced and terrified: the women who weaved and baked and trampled the grapes, the chattering children, the three poets with their lutes and pipes, the chaplain, the artist who had been hired to cover Godfrey's walls with pastoral scenes in bright pigments, the blacksmith and the two jesters.

'Godfrey and his horsemen and his torturers—round them up,' said the earl. 'We will let Sebastian and his people deal with them.'

The Norsemen turned over corpses here and there. All the guardians of the castle were dead. But they could not find Godfrey.

'I think', said Earl Rognvald, 'that Eindred knows something about the escape of Godfrey. I think that Eindred will be richer by a poke or two of Spanish gold after this siege. We will have more trouble from Eindred before we get to Jerusalem and Byzantium.'

9

The soldier-sailors slept long, after the battle.

Next day there was a great feast in the village, that went on till sunset. Sebastian and the villagers saw to it that the fifteen ships were stocked with as much food and wine as they could hold. For, in addition to the hidden stores in the village, there were hogsheads of wine from the cellars of the castle, and great haunches of smoked meat and pork and mutton, poultry and fish.

Earl Rognvald had made a poem while the battle was at its height. Now he recited it, a love song for Ermengarde of Narbonne.

White as snow
White as silver
The lady,

A beauty all whiteness
A kindness
Red as wine.
Another redness, fire
About the castle.
A sharp whiteness, swords.

Einar remarked that they were having their Yule dinner very late that year.

The Lost Sheep

The island had been empty of people for fifty years.

There were a dozen ruins scattered here and there in the island. The sheep sheltered behind those walls in bad weather. I went every summer to shear the flock, and in the autumn to sail them across to Hamnavoe, to the mart there. If possible, I crossed over in the motorboat at lambing time. The weather is often bad at this time of the year, and I have a big farm to run.

If ewes and lambs survive, it is some years the old wisdom of nature that preserves them. More than once, I have found what has been left—a few rags of fleece, a few bones—by the skuas and the hoodie crows.

It is a melancholy island to be in, even for an afternoon. Men and women lived there once that are still spoken about in the other islands for some marvellous thing said or done. There was one famous fiddler. There was a horseman who was sent for from as far away as Shetland and Caithness whenever there were intractable horses. There was the woman who could foretell the weather a month ahead: the fishermen in the island saw to it that she was never short of haddocks and skate. (But at the same time they said, 'Three hundred years ago Meg would have been burned for a witch.')

There had even been a marvellous child in the island, once. In the summer of drought, four or five generations ago, when no rain fell all over Orkney between seed-time and harvest—'the summer of the short corn', it was called—this six-year-old boy went to a stony part of the island and he said, 'They should dig here.' They dug, and water came up sweet and cold.

Those things, and a hundred more, were still remembered about that island, in the fertile islands that lay all about it.

When the last family had left the island, my grandfather had bought it for one hundred pounds, every stone and clod, every shell and seaweed frond down to the lowest ebb. And there my grandfather and my father and now myself grazed a few sheep.

One afternoon, ten years ago and more, I sheltered from a shower in the ruins of the smithy. There was the blackened forge, still. The anvil had been too valuable to leave behind. A few horseshoes hung here and there against the walls. There was a scattering of nails on the bench. I was struck by the shine and sharpness of the nails—they could still have been used for roof-timbers or to build a boat.

I thought, 'Here the island men came together on winter nights to tell their stories.' The stories of that island have passed into the great silence. Something delicate and unique and rich—the spirit of the island—died when Willie the blacksmith closed his door for the last time.

Brightness seeped through the webbed window of the smithy. I could see grey cinders in the forge. The shower was past. I went down in sunshine to my boat on the shore.

There is a retired sailor who rents a small bothy from me down at the shore. He spends most of the time—when he isn't in the village inn drinking—scanning the horizon through his brass telescope.

I don't have much to do with old Ben: he is one of those ancient mariners who tell, over and over, his experiences at sea since he first joined a trawler at Hamnavoe at the age of fifteen. There are about twenty stories in his repertoire. A man gets weary of listening to them over and over again—at least I do. Ben is made welcome at most houses, but he visits most often the farms and crofts where they brew their own ale. So I rarely see him, except when I go down to the bothy to collect the rent.

The winter last year was cold and stormy.

The first television sets had come to the island. They were the latest of the never-ending miracles of science, those half-dozen television sets lately installed in the bigger farms. They held children from their play and old men from their memories in the chimney corner. The poorer folk who couldn't afford to buy television sets would almost beg to spend their evenings in those fortunate houses where the grey images flickered and came and went.

I'm glad to say that the enchantment didn't last. The islanders came to the conclusion that there was probably more fun playing draughts on the kitchen table by lamplight. The fiddle was taken down from the wall again. Cherished books were brought from the wide windowsill and opened with reverence and delight. But while it lasted, even Ben the sailor was under the spell of the television set, going from this house to that.

My wife and three children, I know, would have welcomed a set in our house. I answered their unspoken pleas with a hard look, and silence.

The gales began in late October and seemed to follow each other, with only brief interludes, going in a great wheel through the twelve quarters during November and well into the first half of December. The sun is a dying ember at that time of year in the north. People come out of the bitter winds and gather round those small providences of the sun, the peat-fires on the hearth, the mild radiance of the lamps. (But here again, I'm sorry to say, in most island houses nowadays they get electric light and warmth from the wind generators at the gable-end of the barn.)

There came a knock at the door late one morning. There was a lull that day in the winter-long storm. The sky was a pale blue, but there were battlements of blue-black cloud on the horizon westwards, and that meant snow. The low sun flashed off a quiet sea.

When Ben came in, there were a few snowflakes in his hand. He was carrying his brass telescope.

My wife hastened to make tea for the visitor.

'No,' said Ben, 'I can't stay. I just came to say, one of your sheep in the island has gone over the cliff. She seems all right but there's no way for her to get back.'

Normally, on a winter afternoon, with

darkness due and snow clouds threatening, I would have left the ewe to nature. Let her find her own way to the top. If not—it had happened before, it would happen again. Nature is cruel.

In the end I followed the old sailor down to the shore.

I pushed out the boat, started the motor, and went in a wide arc along the tide-rip to the edge of the small cove in the deserted island. I went at once to the part of the cliff where the ewe had gone over. There was no sign of it on any of the crag-ledges. It had likely lost its footing and fallen into the sea.

The cold sun stood just over the southeast horizon. The snow cloud had come up quickly from the west, and before I knew it I was enveloped in a blizzard. The crystal of the day was broken—a wind began to sough among the barren whin bushes. I was happy about the wind at least. It meant that the snow clouds would be kept on the move. I would not be exiled on the island by a day-long blizzard. I could get home by the light of sunset, or even, if I had to wait that long, by the stars.

Meantime the snow was falling thicker. I would have to shelter, like the flock, behind some wall.

A ruin loomed through the murk, the church.

I assure you, no one has visited the island except myself all this past year. It is a small hump in the sea, that island. Every movement on it is visible from my house across the Sound.

A fire had been lit some time that day against the east wall of the kirk. I could smell the incense of still-smouldering peat. There it was, a fire-black stone with warm ash on it.

There had been a meal too, of a kind. Alongside the fire were the bones of two fish—haddock—and five crusts from a torn loaf.

On the other side of the fire-stone three coins had been left—a shilling, a sixpence, and a penny.

They were honest guests, whoever they were. This payment, I thought, must be for the use of the sanctuary. By right the coins were mine, but I thought it better to leave them there, under the last light and the snow.

As I stood in the kirk porch, the big snow cloud had moved off eastward, and the first star was out over the Atlantic. The air was quiet again. But another blue-black battlement was building up on the western horizon. There would be more snow before midnight. It was cold. I walked quickly down to the boat at the shore.

Ben Smith had stuck a candle in a bottle

in his window. It looked more festive, that flame, than the tinsel-coloured Christmas lights in this farm window and that.

No doubt the sailor had spied all my movements that day on the island of sheep. He came down to meet me. Did I expect to hear a story of some strangers on my island, winter trespassers, and where had they come from, and how had they gotten on to the island, and what did they want there at this time of year? Surely he had seen something through that lucid prism.

All Ben said was, 'A good Yule to you, mister.'

I went on past him without a word, up to my farm that had no tree in the window.

A Boy's Calendar

There was a big calm on the sea in January. Fishing boats left Skibbigoe. While the boats were out the snow came from the north. I could not see barn or byre through the blizzard. The women, in grey shawls, left for the shore. They seemed like a troop of ghosts.

'Stay behind,' said my mother. 'See to the fire.'

How could I keep to the house when my father and brother were in the *Merle*, in danger? I went down to the noust too and hid behind a rock.

'They're blind out there, the boats,' said old Liza. 'It's worse than a storm.'

Sea and land were woven together, one greyness, except for the 'hush-hushing' of small waves on the stones.

Then I saw a vague shape in the sea-grey, and heard the voice of Jock Isbister. The *Sparrow* had felt its way to Skibbigoe. The *Sparrow* came in, laden with haddocks.

More hidden voices, then *Norsk* appeared, her three fishermen coated head to feet in snow. Willie Voe had two baskets, one half full.

The shore of Skibbigoe was a scatter of silver. The blizzard had moved off south, a big blue-black cloud. There was a patch of blue above, and rinsings of sunlight.

We saw the three other Birsay boats making for home. My father's boat, the *Merle*, had only a small catch. But my mother laughed as she handed the men ashore, as if it was a half basket of ringing silver, not fish.

When I got home, the fire was mostly grey ash. But I had a good flame going, under the black broth pot, before my mother and father and brother came home with the fish.

February, I think, is the dreariest month. I trudge, with half a dozen others from the hamlet of North-side, the two miles to school.

Sometimes we put our heads into the wind and rain. Nearly every day our fingers are blue with cold. There is little in the way of fun or banter on February mornings.

Once the minister came by, in his pony and gig, and he drove us to school. 'Study hard,' said he, 'and get on in the world.'

We were too shy to make any reply.

Then one by one we went into the big classroom where a score of pupils were seated.

'Late again,' said Miss MacCulloch.

What lovely flames tossed in the school hearth!

One by one we six North-siders set our peats down, and went quiet as mice to our places.

Miss MacCulloch had written the seven times table on the blackboard. Her apron was white with chalk dust.

Then, at a sign from Miss MacCulloch, we all stood for the *Our Father*.

Why does the whole world seem to be in a rage, in March?

The winds howl from north and west. The women's washing is torn from the line sometimes, and a shirt or a jersey picked up in the next parish.

The crofters fret and complain. It's too stormy for fishing. The winter work in the barn is done. The women rage about this and that. There's little food in cupboard and girnel.

Outside the schoolyard, some of the bigger boys fight with each other. One lies in the last remnant of snow in a ditch beyond the mill, crying.

At nightfall, my mother goes out with a lantern to the byre.

My brother Tom is building a house on a patch of moor that he has drained and dug. In the longer evenings he wheels stones from the new-opened quarry a mile away.

My mother says, 'Your brother is getting married in the autumn, he can't live here with his wife, they need a house to themselves.'

Her mouth had a bitter line when she said that.

Now all the cows of the parish were out on the hillsides, eating the new grass.

There were new lambs in every field, tottering on their legs at first, then leaping high in the air and giving tiny tremulous bleats.

'Help me to set a few stones,' said Tom. 'You'll be well paid.'

'The boy will stay at home and learn his lessons,' said my mother.

When she was out feeding the hens I followed Tom to the growing stonework of his house.

There was a girl standing there, at the half-made gable. 'This is Wilma,' said Tom shyly.

She was a bonny lass, but I let on not to see her, mixing sand in a bucket for cement.

A lark sang, high over Greenay Hill. How could there be so much joy in a small bird like that?

I mixed cement till my arms were sore.

The sun was down. Tom and Wilma still laid stone upon stone.

When I got home, there sat my father in the deep chair, tired after a day's ploughing.

My mother was heating a pot of ale over the fire.

'No supper for you, my lad,' she said, 'till you do your lessons.'

She lit the lamp on the table where my book and jotter were spread.

It's the month of May, a happy time.

After school, after teatime, the boys of North-side, whenever the tide's on the flood, go down to the rocks and fish with wands and hooks for cuithes. Cuithes are stupid fish, they seem to throw themselves on the hooks, time after time. There are thousands of them; soon our basket is brimming.

There will be a fight, for sure, about the division of the fish. But meantime we are happy, hauling the fish on to the rock and easing their jaws from the hooks.

The flood darkens. It is near the full. The sky is all red and yellow and black in the northwest.

Suddenly we hear a plop and a loud cry. Jamie Flett, in the excitement of a cluster of cuithes on his line, has slipped off the rock into the sea. Amid mockery and small cries of concern, he is hauled, dripping, on to the rock. His teeth are chattering. He looks ashamed.

'You'd better run home to the fire,' says Magnus Skeld. 'We'll save your share of fish...'

Outside the North-side houses, in the darkening, we quarrelled about the division of the catch. 'Of course I caught more than you'... 'No, my hooks were never empty, I was watching you, half-an-hour went by and you caught not a single fish'... 'You liar!'... 'Remember Jamie's share'...

A black cat stood mewing piteously beside the hoard of cuithes.

We glared at one another, and shouted, through the fast-gathering shadows.

A door opened. An old woman stood there framed against the lamplight.

'Old Andrew Sinclair is very ill. Think shame of yourselves, making such an outcry.'

The lamps were being lit in every window. In Andrew Sinclair's house the light was low.

We divided the sea-spoils quietly, in equal shares, one share for Jamie Flett.

We threw a cuithe to the black cat.

Bertie Scott, the loudest mouth in our company, the bully, paused at the sick man's house. He strung half a dozen rock-caught fish and hung them on the sneck of the door.

Coming home from the school, we saw a small crowd of men in black suits in the kirkyard. They were drifting to the kirkyard gate now, singly and in small groups. I saw my father lighting his pipe at the gate.

Now there was nobody at the open grave but Mr Farquhar the minister and Fred Sinclair the dead man's son and the gravedigger.

The mourners went their ways home.

In the factor's garden, the bushes were full of white roses. Blackbirds sang from tree to tree. The cows wore coats of black silk, moving here and there among the teeming grass. Dogs barked far and near. The first young corn went in a green flush over the lower slopes.

The minister closed his book and shook Fred Sinclair by the hand, and walked among the labyrinth of tombs to the gate.

Fred Sinclair offered the gravedigger a silver coin.

The gravedigger pocketed the shilling. He spat on his hands and thrust his spade into the red earth beside the grave.

We were very solemn for a while, going home with our schoolbags. But a fine wind of boisterous laughter was going through us as we passed the blacksmith's and the shop.

At the house of mourning the door stood open. We could see a dozen and more men standing inside with glasses in their hands. Fred Sinclair was going round with a whisky bottle.

The dead man's daughter, Bella-Ann, was cutting bread and cheese at the table. 'Ah, he was a good man, Andrew Sinclair,' said an old farmer. 'He was a good ploughman and a good fisherman too...I mind well the time...'

The sea fell lazily on the stones below. The boats were drawn high up on the noust.

There would be no fishing done that day.

A few nights later, I woke up and saw the midsummer fires burning on Ravey Hill and Greenay Hill and, far off, on a hill in the island of Westray.

All of July we were free as the wind and the waves. No school for five weeks.

We flew kites from the top of Ravey Hill whenever the blue air began to surge and dance; and the kite-flying caused a few quarrels among the boys. One kite would go higher than the rest, or kites would collide and tangle with each other.

One cold day we were rifling the pools

for whelks when we saw an old woman going here and there along the tide-mark. Sometimes she shaded her eyes and looked out to sea. Sometimes she turned and looked at the farms and crofts above, and mumbled words through her sunken mouth.

We knew who she was, Old Maddie from the Moorland district. After her man died and her children grew up and went to Australia and South Africa and Canada, first she became forgetful and then her mind began to wander among the old legends that the people told each other on winter nights. Lately she thought she had once been a seal, long ago. Sammy Longaglebe, a young man, had fallen in love with her, and she with him, and she had shed her sealskin and gone to live with him in his croft in the Moorland. And she had learned baking and spinning and butter-making, and brought up six children. Now that she was alone, her only thought was to get back to the seal people. That was why she came to the shore every day. There were seals in plenty, lying on the rocks and splashing in the sea, but they paid no attention to her.

'I think', she told everyone, 'the seals don't want me any more—I'm too old now...' Or she would say, 'I've forgotten the song. If only I knew the seal song, they would take me back. They would have to take me back. But it's no use, no use.'

The boys would frighten each other that Maddie could change a person into a rat or a starling, or a crab, any creature she chose.

We dared Magnus Skeld to go and speak to her.

Magnus said, in a tremulous voice, 'Maddie—Mrs Longaglebe—how old are you?'

She looked at him for a long time. Then she said, 'You'd better be careful, boy. It's dangerous, a bonny creature like you playing on the shore. The seal lasses, they'll come and take you...'

We went back to raking in the pools for whclks, loading our caps with them.

I told my mother and father we had had words with the seal woman on the shore.

'Poor Maddie,' said my father. 'She was born in the Mill, among grain sacks, eighty-five years ago. I doubt if she's put a finger in the sea, ever.'

And my mother said, 'What'll ever become of her, the poor old body?'

We were out in the hayfields, in the sun, day after day, till we were as brown as tinkers. We got all the fields in the district cut before the rain came.

The fiddler began to play.

113

The wedding procession began to move in a long column of pairs—a man with a woman—from the house along the dusty road to the manse.

I had not thought Wilma could be so beautiful in her white dress. My brother Tom looked red-faced and embarrassed in his black suit.

That fiddle of Mark Tait's scared the larks out of the sky that day.

Some old folk lagged far behind in the procession.

On the way back from the marriage ceremony, the fiddle out in front still ranting and rasping, we passed a few old men sitting on a stone dyke, smoking. They hadn't been able to walk all the way. They shouted greetings to Tom and Wilma. Then they joined the tail-end of the procession, hirpling and hobbling on their sticks, remembering weddings of fifty years ago.

To tell the truth, I don't remember much about the feast and the dancing in the big barn. I remember the oat-cake being broken over the bride's head. I remember my father mixing the bride-drink, hot ale and whisky and brown sugar in the wooden 'cog', and how Tom and Wilma carried it among the hundred guests, offering it to the oldest first.

From the house came the smell of

114

stewed chicken and broth. A dozen women were busy there over the fire. Presently, the long table would be laid.

The barn door opened. A tramp called Josh stood outside, rigged in fantastic rags, with his bowl. A chicken leg was put into it, and a buttered bannock. He was given a cup of ale.

Wilma offered me the bride-cog. She looked more like an angel or a princess than a croft lass that night.

I buried my face in the hot sweet spiced drink, and drank and drank.

Soon the barn was a confused wheel of noise and colour.

'Mercy, the boy's fallen,' I heard a voice say from a great distance.

When I woke up in bed, the sun was rising over the islands in the north.

I could hear the fiddles in the barn and the stamp of dancing feet, and occasional barbaric cries from the mouths of the dancers.

Every note, every beat, every cry was like a nail being driven into my skull.

The bere harvest and the oat harvest were cut and stacked.

Anxiously, for days beforehand, the farm folk had stood at their gable-ends studying the sky for signs of storm. One or two old men and women were gifted in weather-prophecy, they could tell the weather for a week to come, a few could prognosticate for a whole season. They took into consideration, for example, the fruitage on the rowan trees and the behaviour of the birds.

Some of the old wise ones said the harvest signs were bad, very bad. They had licked their forefingers and held them up. 'Wind and rain!' old Sophie lamented. 'Wind and rain and a hungry year to come.'

But the harvest was cut and gathered in mellow golden days.

My father sang as he swung his scythe. The sun came flashing off his blade. The crisp corn fell in swathes.

The harvesters with their scythes visited each croft in turn.

The women followed, stooping and binding the sheaves...

We drove in carts to the Lammas Fair in Hamnavoe, setting out at sunrise.

In Hamnavoe, I had not thought there could be so many people in the world. There were tents and booths everywhere, and strange-tongued fairground folk from the south, urging and cajoling.

I remember the mounds of oranges and apples, a blind fiddler wending through the crowds of country folk and town folk and island folk, goldfish in little round bowls, a Negro prince who licked a red-hot poker and said 'sugar', the fortune teller with mystic signs on her booth who crooked a compelling finger at giggling girls: 'Come, I see your husband-to-be in your hand,' preaching men at the fountain, a sweetie stall and an ice-cream stall, a cheapjack with a dazzling tongue.

The crowds surging this way and that bewildered me and delighted me, but I gave a wide berth to a man here and there that staggered and shouted and shafted a whisky bottle.

I had set out with one shilling and sixpence-ha'penny in my pocket. By mid-afternoon I was what my father called 'a bankrupt'.

But the kaleidoscope got more and more enchanting.

At early evening the fair people lit the flares among their stalls and booths, and the harbour water gave the reflections back, undulant and bright and exotic.

I was exhausted with magic and apples, chocolate and the multitude of voices that had sung and laughed and gossiped everywhere that day.

It was a long bumpy road home to Birsay in the cart. I was sick only once, in a ditch at Marwick.

Ezra Black kept the smithy.

The folk complained that he read more books than he hammered horseshoes.

The women complained because the men foregathered in the smithy on winter nights, for story-telling or for arguments about politics (the Boer War) or religion (whether or not the United Presbyterians should unite with the Free Kirk).

One cold October day I was going home from the school and there was Ezra Black in the smithy reading a book at his paraffin lamp.

The warmth of the forge drew me in.

Ezra's eyes through his thick glasses were huge. 'What nonsense did you learn at the school today?' he said.

I told him we had had geography, reading, history and arithmetic.

'I don't suppose they told you anything about Birsay,' said Ezra.

I laughed. What was there to learn about a grey ordinary place like Birsay?

'Let me tell you, boy,' said Ezra. 'Great events have happened in Birsay, and great men have walked on the shores and the hills here... You know that big ruin down in the village.'

Everyone knew that enormous building, that looked like a smashed skull.

'The King of Scotland's son lived there,' said Ezra. 'Earl Robert Stewart. He cemented it with the blood of the

Birsay peasants who laboured to build it for him. And they hewed the stone and dug the well, and the slavery broke hundreds of them.'

Ezra glared at me out of his huge ox-eyes.

'But he reaped his reward, that Robert Stewart. The King had him executed for treason in Edinburgh. There would have been dancing in Birsay that day, I can tell you.'

Everyone said that Ezra was a socialist and an agnostic. Some boys were warned not to go near the smithy, because of the awful ideas that Ezra might put into their heads. But my mother raised no objection. She said that Ezra was a good man at heart.

'But that only happened you might say yesterday,' said Ezra. 'And Robert Stewart was a vagabond of little account... You know that steep green holm off the shore?'

Of course that islet, Brough-of-Birsay, was known to every Birsay-man. Hadn't we waded out to it, coming home from school, a hundred times? Hadn't I once been cut off by the rising tide, and only got home cold and hungry, six hours later when the ebb had set in? My mother had sent me to bed supperless that night.

'Eight hundred years ago,' said Ezra,

'one of the greatest men in all Europe lived there, on that island—Earl Thorfinn the Mighty. He could hold his own with kings, that earl. He challenged the King of Norway on the King's own ship. He rode with King Macbeth of Scotland over the Alps as far as Rome. It says, in the great saga of the islands, that he had a face like an eagle, and his beard was black as midnight. In those days, boy, Birsay was the capital of Orkney, and forby of nine other earldoms in the north and west of Scotland.'

I could hardly believe it. But Ezra Black was a deeply read man, my father always said, and if he had got the education he deserved, Ezra would have ended as a professor in Aberdeen or Ottawa.

'That Earl Thorfinn had two grandsons,' said Ezra. 'Earl Hakon and Earl Magnus they were called. I wouldn't wonder but they went to school with the monks in the Brough-of-Birsay, them and the sons of the other gentry. When they grew to manhood, Earl Hakon had Earl Magnus done to death on the island of Egilsay. That's the way the aristocrats behaved then-a-days. (May it come soon, the rule of the proletariat, boy—that's to say, government by the people for the people—only then will there be peace on earth and enough to eat for every man, black and white and yellow.) They buried Earl Magnus here in Birsay, and after there were a few so-called miracles they proclaimed him a saint. (They were primitive superstitious times, boy—no lamps of reason and progress such as are being lit all over the world today.) So then what did they do but dig the bones of Magnus up and transfer them to Kirkwall. That's why they have St Magnus Cathedral in Kirkwall.'

I wondered at this for a long time.

Ezra's wife Mabel shouted to him from the kitchen indoors that his tea was on the table.

'So that was the decline and fall of Birsay,' said Ezra. 'Kirkwall was the capital from then on. Since then, the only folk of note in Birsay have been a few witches and smugglers and ministers.'

'Do you want your bloody-puddings cold?' cried Mabel from the between door.

'There's one of the witches now,' said Ezra and winked hugely through his thick lens.

As I left for home Ezra said, 'Stick to your books, boy. Get on in the world. Light a lamp here and there, if you can, for the sake of all humanity.'

In November, it seemed that death walked through the parish with his scythe.

Many days, as we trooped home from

the school, we saw the gravedigger at work, either digging a hole or shovelling in last earth over a coffin.

'That was old Maddie that was buried today,' said Mansie Skeld. 'She died at the weekend.'

'Maybe they should have buried her in the sea,' said Bertie Scott. 'Maybe they should have given her back to her own people, the seals.'

One morning, bent over our history primers, we were aware of horses going past the tall school window, and a few gigs and a horse-coach that thundered imperiously along the road.

'Pay attention to the lesson,' cried Miss MacCulloch sharply.

When we were released into the school yard at dinnertime, we saw what the procession was for. Solitary, in a corner of the kirkyard, lay the laird who had died recently in Edinburgh, under such masses of flowers that you might think every garden in Orkney had been plundered. The ceremony was over. The gentry from all over Orkney were mounting their horses. The laird's widow and three daughters were being handed into the coach by the Episcopal minister.

The gravedigger spat on a gold coin and put it in his purse and lit his pipe.

We went home across the fields, to leave

the road free for the horsemen.

One day the fishing-boat *Tern* sailed in on a rising sea with two men in her instead of three. Eddie Ingarth's feet had got entangled in a rope and he had stumbled into the sea. He died soon after they got him in-board again. That was a sad business. Eddie Ingarth had a wife and two small children. The kirkyard was full to overflowing with mourners. Eddie had been a good fisherman and one of the best story-tellers in the alehouse.

The gravedigger gave his fee to the widow. The innkeeper sent three bottles of Old Orkney whisky to the bereft house without charge, so that the old customs be properly observed.

We saw a funeral with only four people present. Two parish-relief men were lifting a boxwood coffin out of a cart. The minister read the service for the dead. The coffin was let down on ropes. A poor-relief man offered a few coppers to the gravedigger who spat on them and put them in his purse. The poor-relief men wheeled the cart away. The minister said another prayer over the open grave of Josh the tramp, and sprinkled on three siftings of earth. The gravedigger lit his pipe.

The lamps were lit early in the houses, in late afternoon.

Where would death strike next?

The elderly sat under the lamps, some with tranquil faces, some with grey uncertain faces.

The old Yule customs were dying out in Birsay and all over Orkney. The ministers had been against them for centuries, as relics of popish superstition. Since the opening of the school and compulsory education, schoolmasters (and now Miss MacCulloch) spoke disparagingly about such idle on-goings. The big progressive farmers would have none of that ignorant nonsense in their houses and byres and barns.

Still some of the older folk spoke kindly about the old observances they had known: the singing of the 'Mary Midder' song over the sleeping children, the candle lit in a cow's skull in every byre, the baking of the yellow sun cakes, the strict prohibition on work of every kind on the eve of St Thomas (the winter solstice)...

One old woman declared that December was a cold dark miserable month now, when even Christmas Day wasn't observed.

The lamps were lit earlier and earlier, in mid-afternoon.

The houses were fragrant with peat smoke.

One afternoon a tinker family came through the first drifting snowflakes and they pitched a tent in a quarry.

An old tinker wife came among the houses. Soup was poured into her pail and cheese and oatcakes and a ham-end were put in her bag. She was a well-known tinker. My father gave her a dram to keep out the cold.

She and her folk, she said, had come, lately, from the island of Westray. A terrible thing had happened there. A foreign ship had gone ashore in the recent storm. At night the ship struck. When the Westraymen went down with lanterns, the shore was strewn with dead bodies. The ship was breaking up fast on the rocks.

There, among all the drowned people— seamen and passengers—they came on a child that still had a little flame of life left in him.

A croft lass carried him up to her hearth.

The foreign infant was thriving, said old Kirstie the tinker, when they had left Westray for the big island.

The name of the wrecked ship was the *Archangel.*

Since there was no way of knowing the child's name, they had christened him Archie Angel.

The Woodcarver

Jock and Liza his wife had a most terrible
fight on the sixth of January, after Jock
had been at the first-footing for five nights
running, and was very grumpy when he
woke up one morning and realised he had
visited every house in the island that kept a
whisky bottle. And now Jock's own whisky
bottle was empty.

Liza hated drink of any kind. She had
been known to pour a full bottle of malt
down the sink when Jock was asleep. That
particular time, ten years ago, they had
heard Liza's screams and Jock's violent
expostulations at the other end of the
island.

This January Liza was almost as mad.

Most of the islanders sided with Liza,
including *all* the women. They knew that
Jock was bone lazy. He could have worked
on the roads, or helped with the lambing
and the harvest. But no, he turned down
every job, and did nothing but wander
about on the beach, finding glass balls and
ships' lifebuoys and sometimes a piece of
sailor's gear.

Certainly they would have starved if Liza

hadn't gone out to scrub the school and the kirk and the laird's house.

Jock had a kind of bothy between his house and the sea. In it he stowed such treasures as the sea cast ashore. Ten years ago he had dragged a brass lamp out of a shore wave, and it was the brightest thing in that grotty hut, even when it wasn't lighted in summer. On winter days it made the bothy a cave of enchantment.

To this wretched hut Jock went whenever there was bad blood between him and Liza. He might cook a crab or some sausages in the pot, on top of the red throbbing stove. But he wouldn't go back to Shore-end (that was the name of their house) till Liza, after maybe three or four days, came and knocked at the bothy door. Then, when he said in his gruff voice, 'What's ado?' Liza would enter with a plate of hot buttered bannocks and a thermos of soup. Then Jock knew that another peace treaty had been signed, and it was safe enough for him to sit beside his own fire and smoke his pipe.

If you had seen them at such a time, you'd have sworn that a more contented couple never lived on Njalsay island.

There was a wild storm in the middle of January and Njalsay's six fishing-boats just made it home in time, but a fishing-boat *Beagle* from Selsay isle had been caught between wind and ebb and overset. The old fisherman had managed to struggle ashore but his son was drowned.

Jock knew that old fisherman Tom Richan, and he grieved for him.

The sea had overset richer game then *Beagle,* judging by the stuff strewn on the beach two mornings later—a mast and two benches and a sodden wallet and a bleached sea-boot and the stern and rowlock of a ship's boat.

Jock dreaded finding bodies along the tide-line but there were none. Some bodies came ashore later in Shetland.

(The truce had not been signed yet after Jock's awful carry-on between Hogmanay and the sixth of January. He was still banished to the shed.)

His latest sea bounty was heaped outside the bothy, with a bit of net over it.

Inside, Jock grieved for Tom Richan and his drowned son. There were fish boxes everywhere—they were the sole furniture of the bothy.

Jock found that he was holding a six-inch nail with a sharp point on it. He took up a fish box and sank the nail into the wood, then he drew a fluent line that might be a boat's hull.

He was so hungry that he carved on the wood all afternoon. In the middle of the task he lit the ship's lamp and went on with his work.

When it was pitch dark outside, Jock had carved a great curling wave with a fishing-boat hung perilously in it.

Jock was so pleased with the work that he had to show it to somebody—Liza for example. But Liza had forbade him the house—he only realised that when he was half-way up the path.

Somebody was there, in the moonless dark, coming to meet him. It was Liza, with the plate of new bannocks and the thermos of soup: the peace offering.

'Mercy!' cried she. 'What a fright you gave me!'

They went inside the house together. It was such a clean warm ordered place, compared to his hovel!

Before he had his supper, Jock showed Liza his carving.

She looked at it and shook her head—she didn't think much of it.

In February dark snow clouds came from the north and swallowed the island. Then, when the blue returned and the sun glanced from a corner of the last snow cloud, the isle of Njalsay was transfigured, all immaculate white humps and hollows. Icicles hung from the eaves of Shore-end, flashing like crystal in the sun. Liza had to break the thin ice on the water-barrel. The children were going by to the school:

129

the light of sky and snow seemed to purify their faces, and their breath smoked as on they danced to the school bell's bronze summons.

But even Jock and the blacksmith and the postman looked other-worldly and beatified as they trudged along the drifted-under road.

Liza's cheeks were like two polished apples.

The glory lasted only two days. Clouds covered the sun again, only this time they came in great hordes and clusters from the west, and they dropped warm Gulf Stream rain all day and all night.

The island next morning looked like some old tramp that had slept in a ditch—mud and slush everywhere. The lovely garment of snow was reduced to a few rags and tatters in the lee of dykes, and on the upper slopes of the hill Fea.

No point in Jock going to the beach with his bag. The snow had come in windless weather and now in this hideous thaw the sea was grey and calm.

Jock and Liza got on well in the snow and the thaw.

At last the rain clouds took themselves off.

Jock took his coat off the hook in the lobby.

'Where are you making for?' said Liza a

bit tartly. It was possible the old fool might make for the village pub, to hear how the island had fared in the snow—whether any sheep had been smoored, whether any of the crofts in the valley had managed to dig their way out.

Liza knew that Jock had no money, but he had perfected a talent for being made welcome at any drinking circle. He had a great hoard of stories that the men of Njalsay never tired of, and some Saturday nights he could sing till the rafters of the pub re-echoed.

'I'm off to see if the thaw's gotten in to the bothy,' said Jock.

That was all right, thought Liza. The wonder was that the hovel had a roof at all, so eaten it was with dry rot and rain and the Atlantic salt.

'Dinner's at one,' said Liza.

One o'clock came and went and Jock's bowl of broth got cold on the table.

He knew the time—he had an alarm-clock (another seagift) on the shelf.

With every minute that passed, Liza grew ever more certain that the creature was sitting at the pub fire, drinking whisky that the island drouthies—poor creatures all—had bought for him.

Well, let him thole his hangover in that old shed, in utter misery! She would offer him neither fire nor board.

But when Liza went to feed the hens, the smoke was rising out of his lum, and she heard an urgent scratching and rasping from the interior.

She had half a mind to let him wait till hunger drove him in to his cold soup and beef and tatties.

But he hadn't gone to the pub, that was one thing to be glad about. Liza went between lingering patches of dirty snow and ice to the bothy.

There he was, humming to himself—a good sign, that—and scoring the bottom of a fish box with a big nail. There it was, another carving—a cluster of curves on the wood.

'Your dinner's been on the table an hour,' said Liza.

He said nothing. She might never have existed.

He scored deep into the wood with his nail.

'Come when you're bidden!' Liza cried, and the bite in her voice was enough to make the six-inch nail clatter on the floor.

The humming stopped. Jock was angry. 'You could have spoiled it,' he cried. He picked up his nail. 'I'll come in when it's dark,' he said. 'You go about your own business.'

It had all the makings of a first-class row.

Liza shut the bothy door and went back to the house...

Later, by lamplight, he ate his supper like a famished wolf. But every now and again he would stop the champing of his jaws and sit for a few minutes in a trance. Then he would cut another slice of cheese and put it on his oatcake.

'The few snowdrops beside the gate,' Jock said. 'I never saw anything so bonny. The earth's coming alive again...'

Liza had not heard talk the like of that from him before. Maybe he was going out of his mind.

Snowdrops!

There was maybe some connection between the frail white flowers in the lee of the garden dyke and that cutting and scratching on the fish box. 'But the carving is no more like a snowdrop than my nose is like the Rock of Gibraltar,' thought Liza... Still, his cutting and scraping was better than guzzling beer in that den of iniquity, the inn.

The men round the pub fire wondered what was keeping Jock away. It was now the third week of March and he had never darkened the inn door.

'It looks like old Liza's got him under control at last,' said Sandy the ploughman.

They considered, one after the other,

nodding their heads, that the inn was a poorer place lacking Jock's stories and songs.

'There was that storm at the weekend,' said the inn keeper, Mr Smellie. 'Lots of pickings in the ebb for him.'

'No,' said Jerry the fisherman. 'If Jock gets back to his shed with a full sack, he dumps it and makes straight for this place—a dram and a pint or two.'

It was a wonder.

The drinkers were mostly farmers and crofters. The loam of the ploughing was on their tongues. They smelt of horses. Whisky never tasted so good as after a day making furrows.

They would all have gladly bought Jock a drink.

'Poverty's no crime,' said Sigurd of Dale.

Sandy, the ploughman of Skaill—he and Jock had sat together in the classroom forty years before—thought he would call by at Shore-end on his way home.

Like nearly all the drinkers, he was scared of Liza's tongue; so he did not dare pass her window.

'Oho,' thought Sandy, coming round the curve of the shore road, 'they've fallen out again...' For, besides the light in the house, there was smoke rising from the bothy chimney.

When Sandy cautiously opened the door, there sat Jock smoking his pipe and looking at a fish box as though it contained ocean treasures. Nor did he greet his old drinking friend.

In the lamplight, Sandy saw that the surface of the fish box was ruined with knife marks.

Sandy looked closer. There seemed to be the crude outlines of a plough and a horse.

Little splinters and curves of wood, and a six-inch nail, lay on the flagstone.

Still Jock said nothing.

Sandy thought of going to Shore-end to ask Liza if anything ailed Jock. But in the end he didn't go. The whisky smell of his breath was too strong.

No one in Orkney knows from one day to the next what the weather will be. The North Atlantic climate is like that—one day is wind and flung spindrift, the next is loveliness beyond compare (all crystalline and the blue sky and the bluer sea out of which the sun mints a myriad golden coins), and the day after that sullen, with a dark sea haar blotting out the near islands and the horizon beyond... No wonder the main topic of conversation when islanders meet is the weather: what gift or bane would it deal out in the next day or

135

two? After twenty generations, they had a shrewd notion what would come.

One day in the rainy April of that year, when Liza was away cleaning the school, Jock found a pound note tucked away behind the china dog on the mantelpiece—money that Liza was keeping to buy necessaries from the grocery van that stopped on the road outside every Saturday morning.

It was one of those Aprils bounteous with rain and bright days, and this month the island was fretted with daffodils—it seemed that every piece of tilth and pasture was stitched together with those harbingers of spring.

Jock took a devious route to the inn in case he should meet Liza returning from her cleaning of the school. And guiltily he laid the pound note on the bar counter and asked for a dram and a pint.

The only customer that afternoon was Captain Scarf, a retired skipper, who frequently threw people off balance with the bluntness of his speech. The captain had lost a leg in the war and when the pain of the lost leg was more than he could bear he could be particularly brutal and direct.

Jock invited Captain Scarf to have a drink with him. (In those days you could buy a fair amount of drink for a pound.)

The old skipper's beard twitched. He said, 'I wouldn't drink with you, man. Have you no shame? Spending your life scratching in the ebb for lost cargoes. Living off the pain and misery of seamen. You're the worst kind of scavenger, man.'

Jock was so taken aback by this abuse that he pocketed the pound note and left the inn, the flame in his throat unquenched.

'A water rat,' Captain Scarf was saying to the innkeeper. 'A hoodie crow!'

Jock was shaken and ashamed. He hurried home to restore the money to its rightful place. But Liza was before him. When she was out getting peats, Jock put the pound note behind the china dog.

He thought about what the old skipper had said, and the reproof sank deep.

Of course most of his sea-gleaning had nothing to do with wrecked ships. What was he to do, all the same, if one of those tragedies happened under the horizon? Others would come and take the pickings, and they didn't know where to look or what to look for. Besides, it was bred in his bones that whatever was found on the tide-mark was a gift from the mighty mother the sea—who, if she gave lavishly with one hand, took her toll with the other cold indifferent cruel hand.

Jock was discovering that he could

cancel, to a great extent, shame and guilt with his fish boxes and his six-inch nail.

In the last of the light he carved a ship, well freighted, going from one shore of corn and fleeces to another shore of gaunt faces and hungry hands outstretched.

It was the biggest carving he had ever attempted, and before it was finished he had to light the lamp.

Liza had called thrice—the last time angrily—that his supper was on the table.

In spite of the vernal quickening everywhere—the bounty of daffodils and larks and new lambs—Liza was ill thrawn too that day.

Jock sat down to his supper of oatcakes and cheese and made no answer to her barbed talk.

He exulted silently in the work he had done.

The laird of the island was a progressive young man newly out of Cambridge, who had a genuine interest in the welfare of his islanders.

Nothing is secret for very long in such a community. Word came to Mr Martin-Rowland up at the Hall of the eccentric behaviour of one of his people, Jock Sigurdson. The young laird was interested in the arts. One fine morning in May he drove down to Shore-end. The sight of him through the window threw Liza into a panic—it was her washing day, the room was full of steam and damp clothes drying before the fire, a terrible stramash—besides, her face was flushed and she was soapsuds up to the elbows. Neither she nor the house was in fit state to entertain the fine-spoken young man.

She decided not to let him in.

It was her husband he wanted to see, he told her on the doorstep, in such fine stylish language that she only managed to take in a word or two here and there.

Jock—there was no doubt that it was Jock he wanted to see.

From inside the bothy came the scraping and scratching of the six-inch nail wounding the wood.

Liza pointed at the bothy door, wordlessly (lest her island accent might grate on Mr Martin-Rowland's ears) and closed the door on him.

No more would Jock let him cross his threshold. ('A strange old couple,' thought the laird, 'in this island noted for hospitality and courtesy'...) 'I'm very busy,' said Jock. ('And this,' thought the laird, 'from reputedly the laziest man in Njalsay.') The laird managed to see over Jock's shoulder five fish boxes with carvings on them. They were, no doubt about it, pieces of genuine primitive art.

'So I'll be getting on with my work,' said Jock, 'if you have nothing in particular to see me about.'

On the bench was Jock's work-in-progress, a shoal of fish swimming into a net. Certain kinds of fish throng the Sound, in silver swarms, at 'the first drink of the May flood'.

'I'm honoured to have an artist in my island,' said Mr Martin-Rowland.

'An artist?' said Jock. 'Not me, I just notch and nag away at a fish box now and then, to get away from the wife.'

'I'd like to buy that one of the boat in the big wave. It's nearly as good as Hokusai,' said the laird.

'They're not for sale,' said Jock, and closed the door against him.

The laird's father would soon have brought those insolent tenants to heel, but Timothy Martin-Rowland was a progressive, liberal-minded young man.

That same day he wrote to a friend of his who was art critic of a quality newspaper, inviting him to the island for a summer break. He promised good trout fishing and shooting, but said nothing about the woodcarver.

At the same time he wrote to an art dealer in Edinburgh, asking for proper woodcarving tools to be sent to Jock as soon as possible, and a stack of the best quality wood.

That night, at the supper table, Liza seemed worried. Such boorishness, shutting *two* doors against that nice young man. People in the past had been evicted for less.

Jock thought what a fool he had been, not selling one or two carvings to the laird. If he had gotten a fiver in his hand, he could have bought drink on Friday for all the fishermen and ploughmen of Njalsay! The truth was, he admitted to himself, he had been thrown into confusion by that sudden arrival at his mouse-and-spider-and-flea-infested ruckle.

June was a dull rainy month. It sometimes happens that way. The sun was there, behind all those clouds, in its high meridian. It never gets dark, a few shadows cluster about midnight, then the fountain of light wells up over the north-east horizon.

But this year the early dawns, morning after morning, were seepings of grey light only.

Some days, at noon, the sun would appear between two clouds, and the island would glow like an emerald in the steel and sapphire sea.

The farmers complained—too much rain, too little sun.

There wasn't much wind either to dry the oats and barley.

Poor weather for beachcombing, too. Jock got odds and ends out of the ebb. But one day two big battens of wood came lippering in on the flood. Jock sold them to Thomson the joiner for two pounds. He let the glass balls and broken creels lie where they were, and he took a roundabout way to the inn. It must be recorded with sorrow that he stayed at the bar till midnight.

Liza sat at home, 'gathering her brows like gathering storm'. There they stood on the table, Jock's two boiled eggs grown cold as sea stones.

Once, at ten o'clock, Liza put down her knitting and went out to the bothy to see if the creature was sitting there with his secret bottle.

But no: the hovel was empty. The carved fish boxes were stacked on the bench.

Leaning against Jock's bench was his latest piece of tomfoolery—a blazing sun cut deep into a Buckie fish box...Liza saw this in the last ebbings of light. She had a fleeting impression that the bothy was a place of brightness and fruition.

'What nonsense!' said Liza.

Then she had a sudden impulse to take

an axe to all those carved fish boxes. It would serve him right, the vagabond.

Liza went back to the house and put the kettle on for her hot-water bottle.

Mercifully she was asleep when Jock fumbled his way into the house much the worse of drink.

One day in July the post van stopped outside Shore-end and Freddy Hoy delivered two big parcels. They were registered parcels; Liza had to sign for them.

Jock was poking about in the rockpools a mile away, out of sight.

Liza untied the knots; such fine thick string would come in handy for future use. So would the generous sheets of brown paper, and the city-smelling cardboard boxes.

In one box was a set of new tools, all clean sharp-tempered steel and new varnished wood handles; and, in the other, wooden boards of different sizes.

What was the use of such strange things? Who could have sent them? There was no letter or bill inside; there was the trade name of an Edinburgh art dealer on the side of the boxes.

It must be a mistake.

It was a good summer day over the island. A wind from the sea surged through the green corn. Under the cliffs in the west the six island fishing-boats were lifting their creels.

Liza wondered about the mysterious parcels all the time she was slicing up onions and carrots and tatties and neeps to put into the rib of beef simmering in the soup pot over the stove.

Jock came up from the shore, with four fish boxes (jetsam) under his arms, just as Liza was ladling the broth into the bowls.

He came out of the sun and wind looking as tanned as a tinker. The sea glitter had put an added burnish on his face.

Liza nodded at the two parcels and their contents.

Jock glanced at them, then sat down to three bowls of soup, followed by beef and tatties golden with butter.

Then he pushed the woodcarving tools and the well-prepared surfaces under the box-bed, and he never looked at them or referred to them again.

Liza asked over and over what they were for and who could have sent them.

He gave her no answer. He went out to the bothy to smoke his pipe in silence.

The incenses of summer-salt and corn-wafted into the bothy.

The sun was westering in a glory of crimson and jet and primrose.

144

A lark sang, high and invisible, over Shore-end.

Jock sharpened his six-inch nail on the whetstone and before dark he cut a barley stalk into a fish box.

It was when Jock was making merry in the whisky tent at the agricultural show that the bearded stranger came looking for him.

He had called first at Shore-end. When Liza opened the door, he had asked if a Mr John Sigurdson lived here.

Liza had a brow on her like thunder that day. Brusquely she indicated the showground on the other side of the island, beside the village. Sounds of music and merriment came faintly on the wind. Liza said nothing—she just stabbed with her finger, fiercely, in the direction of the field full of festive country folk.

The bearded man, in a very posh accent, said something about 'works of art, wood engravings'—what he said conveyed nothing to her. It might have something to do with the drunken thing and the fish boxes that he was forever idling over with that big nail.

She nodded coldly towards the bothy.

The door stood open. The young bearded stranger went inside.

Liza, throwing crusts to her hens a few

145

minutes later, heard the man moving about in the bothy. Sometimes the man gave a low whistle-a minute later he would say, 'Well well well', and again, 'Astonishing', or 'Marvellous', or 'Oh, I say, would you look at *this!...*'

There were eight boxes set against the wall. The eighth was 'work-in-progress'; but a sickle and a stook of corn seemed to shout with joy from the unfinished carving.

The stranger gathered from what the grim-faced old woman had said that the woodcarver was at the outdoor rustic festival a mile away.

He walked there with long urgent strides.

Inside the gate, in the square green field, there were horses and thick-fleeced sheep and black ponderous bulls and country folk going laughing among the fiddle music and the tug-o'-war contests and the swing boats and the flower stalls and the tea and cake tents.

The young Londoner stopped this islander and that, enquiring after John Sigurdson.

A strange community! Nobody seemed to know John Sigurdson.

'The woodcarver,' he prompted. A slow shaking of the head, again and again.

At last someone—it was Sandy the ploughman—seemed to understand. He pointed at the big marquee out of which much shouting and singing emerged. And Sandy laughed till the tears came...

On his way to the whisky tent, the stranger met his friend Mr Martin-Rowland the laird.

'The artist,' he said, 'I'm told he's in there.'

The laird shook his head sadly and pointed to a very tipsy man being led out of the field by two policemen.

It was the artist. It was Jock.

The bearded art critic went back to the inn where he was staying overnight and he wrote an account of what he had experienced in the island that day—most of it was about a set of fish boxes with carvings on them.

By early September, the smouldering rage of Liza had died down.

That her man should be arrested, incoherent and legless with drink, before the whole island! That he had been taken to the town and clapped in jail there for one whole night! That the magistrate had fined him one pound next morning for being 'drunk and incapable'!

The shame of it put a few more white hairs on Liza's head.

Jock spent many days and nights in his bothy. Then he was let back to the fire and board of Shore-end again. A few words were exchanged.

Then the *Orkney Herald* came to the island, containing a report of the case, and Liza's cooling rage was blown into flame again—and Jock spent a few more contented days in the bothy, living on boiled tatties and cabbage, and carving another fish box.

The evenings were getting cold, now in autumn.

It had occurred to Jock that he could make his carvings more interesting by a dab of tar here and there, and a splash of white paint. The snowdrop he had carved in February was none the worse for its little coat of light...

Now Jock carved the outline of Njalsay as a fisherman might see it from a mile out at sea—a bold shape rising to the crest of the one hill, Fea. One side of the island he painted black, the other white. The sun over Njalsay was likewise divided into white and black.

He had no sooner finished this work when the door opened and Liza stood there with a thermos of soup and a plate of fish and tatties enriched with little rills of butter.

It was the peace offering, again.

Jock went so far as to kiss her on her russet cheek.

'Less of that,' said Liza.

That evening Jock sat beside the fire indoors.

It was the equinox.

Through the window the great star-wheel was beginning to brighten winterwards. But now—tonight—there was perfect balance, the fruitfulness of summer in equipoise with the winter purgation of snow and darkness.

Jock felt the wonder of it in his bones.

Jock and Liza had hardly finished their suppertime porridge when there was the sound of a car stopping outside, then a loud knock at the door.

It was the young laird. He laid a thick glossy magazine on the table and said in his loud posh voice, 'Well done, well done. Read this.'

He was out and off before Liza could offer him a cup of tea.

Jock had, of course, gone to school but now he had almost forgotten how to read.

Liza thumbed through the pages till she found the article. First there was a big picture of Jock looking scruffy and unkempt, in rubber boots and a patched coat, poking about in the rockpools. The legend above said, in large letters, ISLAND WOODCARVER OF GENIUS.

Liza spelt out the text as best she could,

though many of the phrases were strange and meaningless. Indeed the whole thing was a farrago... 'A remote island far in the north...a tumbledown wooden shack...by the light of one cracked window a collection of fish boxes marvellously illuminated by the untaught genius of the island beachcomber...the essential life of a simple community forever celebrated in primitive engravings...a source of wonder and perpetual refreshment to city dwellers sated with artificial modes of existence... Here is the crude anonymous life-giving word, the fertility dance, the primitive celebration of growth, fruition, and death... I sought an interview with the artist but on that particular day he was too entranced by communal Dionysian rites to communicate...I learned the simple life story from his fellow islanders...' There followed a small biography of Jock, depicting his poverty, his lifelong dedication to his 'daemon' which kept him from island occupations like fishing, crofting, roadwork or being employed at the inn or on the ferryboat... 'So,' concluded the article, 'he has nurtured and guarded his talent lifelong until now...'

At the end of the reading, Jock was too shy and shaken to say a word.

'I never heard such bruck in my life,' said Liza.

150

Through the window the great star-wheel turned above the black bothy with its fish boxes, and above Njalsay with its waters and tilth and ancient tumuli; and the hemisphere from Spitzbergen to Casablanca leaned with its star-wheel into winter.

It was cold in the first days of October.

Jock carved an apple and a fiddle on a fish box—they celebrated happy Hallowe'ens when he was a boy sixty years ago.

The door opened and in came Leslie Arnison who had the first motorcar in Njalsay and had lately made himself a wireless set.

'There was a man speaking about you on the wireless last night, Jock,' said Leslie Arnison, 'saying what a great man you are with your carvings.'

'Go away,' said Jock. 'I'm busy.'

When Jock went in for his dinner of mealy puddings and clapshot, he had hardly sat down when the postman came on his bike, and he laid a pile of letters on the table. A letter was a rare thing at Shore-end.

Liza spelled her way through the letters. At last she said, 'You've stirred up a fine hornet's nest with your cuttings and scrapings!'

151

In a way Liza seemed pleased. She carried off the letters to show to Bella Wilson in the croft of Anders, next along the shore.

Jock found a half-crown under the china dog on the mantelpiece.

'Working with wood', said Jock to the innkeeper, 'makes a man thirsty.'

Then he sat down next the barrel with his dram and his ale.

The moon was up when he wandered off home.

The door was locked. It was, again, the bothy for Jock.

He was in swinish sleep when the group from the arts society in Kirkwall called to see him next morning. They had hired a boat specially.

'He isn't here,' said Liza coldly. 'He's seeing to the pigs somewhere...'

But no one on Njalsay had known of Jock ministering to pigs before.

The arts society lunched at the inn, hoping that they might see the genius in the bar. 'The only pigs Jock knows are pigs of ale at the peat-cutting in May.'

Then the arts society members had to hurry to get back to Kirkwall before it got dark.

They left money with the innkeeper to buy Jock a bottle of whisky, in token of their admiration.

Jock was still exiled in the bothy when the man with the foreign accent came one day. Liza had tried to head him off but the young man seemed to know by instinct where true artists live, in garret or in cellar.

Jock liked the dealer at once, though it was hard to know what he was saying. He went slowly among the carvings, lingering over this one and that.

Jock put a piece of driftwood in the stove, in showers of sparks.

At last the dealer said, 'Look, sir—what do you say?—I'm offering you fifty pounds for the lot.'

Jock backed away as if the man had struck him across the face. 'All that money!' he cried. 'Oh no no, I could never do that! I wouldn't be able to sleep at night. Did you say fifty pounds? Oh never! I'd be richer than the laird.'

The nice young man, Mr Rosenstein, took a little bag from his case—it chimed like a bell—and he solemnly counted out gold sovereigns on the workbench.

He stopped, smiling, after he had laid out twenty-five gold coins.

Jock stood looking at the treasure, bewildered.

Then, like a magician, the art dealer delved once more into his little bag.

The October sun came in at the window,

and took flashings from the array of sovereigns.

Jock was speechless.

The young man seemed content with the impression he was making.

He reached round to his hip pocket and brought out a silver spirit flask. He unscrewed it and offered it to Jock.

And Jock put it tremblingly to his lips.

At that moment it was as if an earthquake hit the bothy.

Liza stood there, rampant!

She knocked the silver flask from Jock's mouth. She rounded on Mr Rosenstein and ordered him out of the bothy. She shook her great bunched fist under his nose. The young man blanched. He had never seen such rage in his life.

'I'll make it a hundred pounds,' he stammered at last.

Liza pointed with a passionate forefinger at the ferry-boat *Rinansay* lying at the pier.

'Off with you!' she cried. 'Get back where you came from! Take your money and your drink. Why can't you and the likes of you leave poor folk alone?'

The man gathered his fifty sovereigns and left hurriedly.

'Quite right,' said Jock. 'He was trying to make a fool of me. Fifty pounds indeed!'

'Your herring and tatties will be ready in five minutes or so,' said Liza and went back to the house.

Jock was having a bit of difficulty over the carving of the October fiddle. But he thought at last he could see a way of doing it, so that it would begin to sing and cry with joy out of the wood.

In the month of November a few of the old folk and 'the trowie bodies' of Njalsay died.

Jock went to all the funerals in the kirkyard, and afterwards in the bereaved croft-houses he drank the memorial whisky, and then there were slow grave elegies uttered by farmers and fishermen, praising the dead person and lamenting the loss.

And again the chief mourner would fill the bowl with whisky and pass it from hand to hand, from mouth to mouth.

If only it had stopped there...

But a few of the mourners called at the inn afterwards. That always happened. And Jock was always there—he genuinely grieved when one of the islanders died, and wanted him or her to be celebrated in the ancient fashion, with barley and ballads in prose.

Apart from the funeral feasts, November was a bleak time for Jock.

Liza forbade him the house. He had to

155

sleep in the bothy several times in his black funeral clothes.

Much of the driftwood was damp and wouldn't burn in the stove.

He lived for days at a time on kale and tatties.

The farmer of the Glebe turned up a Stone Age cist on his land. It contained a skull and some bones. The schoolmaster, who was an amateur archaeologist, was very excited.

Jock went with a few fishermen to see the tarnished skull.

The schoolmaster held it up to the weak November sun. 'Alas poor Yorick,' he said.

The skull gave Jock a subject for the next carving. November was the month of souls.

Some days there seemed to be more folk in Njalsay kirkyard than on the island of the living. It was cold weather. People kept to their fires.

'Well,' said Jock, 'if I'm kept in that bothy much longer I'll be a skull myself.'

The good old farmer of Sudheim died. Jock stood among a flock of mourners in the kirkyard and afterwards at the black-coated circle of celebrants in the farm kitchen at Sudheim.

For Jock the whisky made beautiful the mystery of life and death.

156

When Jock and the mourners went slowly down to the village, they saw a fine yacht lying at anchor in the bay, with stars-and-stripes aloft.

Jock decided not to go to the inn but to go home instead and make his peace with Liza. Who was to know how much longer either of them would live? 'All flesh is grass,' the minister had said that afternoon. How terrible, to die unforgiving and unforgiven!

Coming round the shore road, Jock saw, in the first shadows, Liza taking in peats at the end of the house.

'Away, you drunken vagabond!' she shouted. 'Getting drunk at a funeral—who ever heard the like! Be off, you villain.'

There was nothing else for it. The stove wouldn't light in the bothy, and there was no oil for the brass lamp. Jock lit a candle stuck in the neck of a rum bottle.

With swift pure incisions Jock carved a skull on the eleventh fish box. He put a splash of tar here and there.

'Alas, poor Howie,' he said, naming the good old farmer who had been buried that afternoon.

Then, cold and hungry, Jock set out for the village a mile away...

Behind him, the candle burned low among the wood shavings and tarry rags.

The bar was full of strangers when Jock

got there. The innkeeper pointed to Jock. Then the strangers were all round him in a surge. They put glass after glass of whisky in his hand, and their strange nose-twanging voices were loud with welcome and praise. The man who seemed to be their leader wore a sailor-cap. He put his arm round Jock's shoulder (an unheard of familiarity in Njalsay.) 'At last!' he said. 'I thought we'd have to sail away and never see you. But here you are. Give the genius another Scotch!'

The half-dozen men had come from the American yacht anchored in the bay, and this man was the owner.

After the fifth whisky the inn began to rock gently about Jock like a ship in a rising wind—and his spirit (after the melancholy of the day) surged in response.

He was aware that the nautical stranger was uttering golden words, but he only got a phrase now and again, so boisterous the barleycorn storm was beginning to blow up in his blood.

'Gonna put you on the map... Exhibitions in the best galleries, London, New York, Paris...No more beachcombing for you, John. You're gonna be rich, in no time at all you can buy this hostelry and the whole island...John, I'm proud to meet you... Landlord, give the great artist another whisky, sure make it a double...'

Jock had to sit on the stool, for now the inn was lurching and yawing in a full westerly gale.

Still he hadn't said a word.

The rich American was saying '...Tried to see your works today, John... No way. That's sure a fierce lady you have guarding your treasure... Said you were in the graveyard—gloomy way to talk—I thought maybe you'd passed on... Asked to see the carvings anyway. Nothing doing. Told us we were trespassing. She'd have the law on us... Told us never to come back again, never this side of time... We had pretty heavy hearts, John, standing back here at the bar drinking to the death of a great artist... And here you turn up, as large as life... Oh John, are we glad to see you!... Give the genius another glass of Scotch!... Now, John, how about showing us your work, eh?... Yeah, tonight, it'll have to be tonight, we gotta sail first light... What I'm hoping is, you'll let me take the priceless collection home with me in the yacht.'

They got a lantern from Smellie the innkeeper to light them the dark road to Shore-end. Jock went in front, in a kind of broken dance. He was going to be richer than Carnegie or Rockefeller! The island lurched all about him, like a galleon freighted with ingots.

159

There was a flickering and a flaming in the sky as they rounded the ness.

The Yankees said it must be the northern lights. 'Would you look at that?...'

But when Jock came in view of Shore-end, he saw that his bothy was ablaze from floor to rafters.

'What did you leave that candle burning for', said Liza, 'among all the tar and wood shavings?'

Liza seemed to be untroubled by the tragedy. She sounded pleased, in fact.

'Get to bed, you old fool,' she said gently.

The Americans turned and went back, lantern-splashed, through the fields.

Jock saw no point in hammering and nailing a new shed before next April or May, at least.

It took him three days to recover from the drunken dream of gold that had ended in fire and wreckage.

There were only a few hours in the brief December light for collecting wrack. There had been Atlantic storms—there was a generous strewment of planks and battens along the tide-mark. The new bothy might even be better than the fire-gutted one.

He found at three o'clock in the afternoon, just as the sun was going down into the Atlantic, a fish box bleached and gnawed by the sea.

The only thing he had managed to salvage from the burning bothy was his six-inch nail.

He lit the lantern in the byre—for Liza allowed no woodsplinters in her clean house—and almost before he was aware he had carved a great pulsing star on the fish box.

It seemed to Jock that the star was brighter than the lantern-glow.

The work had lit a star in his own darkling winter blood.

What could he do with this box?

Liza had always refused to have his carvings inside the door of the croft.

He could sell it, since the magazine article and wireless programme and the art dealer and the millionaire Yankee yacht, for a bottle of Old Orkney malt to Smellie the innkeeper, surely.

Instead, Jock found himself in the dark night taking the road to the kirk.

It came into his mind that it was Christmas Eve.

Jock had never been inside the kirk since his mother had dragged him there, a boy in his Sabbath suit, sixty years since.

He might have known it—the kirk door was locked.

A few snowflakes whirled about him.

Jock set the fish box with the star on it at the door of the kirk and came away.

Three Old Men

The old man came out of his house and it was a dark night. A few snowflakes drifted on to his head.

'Well,' he said, 'I don't know why I want to leave the fire on a cold night like this. I want to get to the village but why I don't remember.'

He guessed his way along the track going down from the hill, and once he stumbled and almost fell into the wet ditch.

'Well, thank you, staff, for keeping me on my feet,' said the old man to his stick. 'A fine thing, if they found us in the morning, you and me in a drift in the ditch, as stiff and cold as one another.'

The old man laughed, and he went slowly down the cart road from the hill to the village. He felt happy, though now the snow was in his beard, and he struck out with his staff and startled a star from a wayside stone.

At the crossroads, half-way to the village, a shadow lingered. The shadow declared itself to be a man, because there was the small flame of a match being applied to a pipe. The face shone fitfully once or twice and was part of the night again.

'What's an old man like you doing out in a night like this?' said the voice at the crossroads, and the seeker in the darkness recognised Ben, the retired skipper, from the far end of the island. They had sat in the same classroom at the village school, but then they hadn't seen each other for thirty years, the time Ben was at sea, and now only occasionally at the island regatta or the agricultural show.

'The truth is,' said the old man from the hill, 'I don't rightly remember. I know I have some errand to the village, and maybe it'll come back to me before I get to the bridge.'

'Well,' said Ben, 'we might as well walk on together. I expect it's drink you're after, to keep out the cold. We can hold each other up on the way home.'

The two old men laughed. The skipper had a smell of hot rum on his breath. Could he be wanting more grog in the inn?

'I just thought', said Ben, 'I would like to stretch my legs under the stars. Only there's not a star to be seen. It's as black as the ace of spades.'

The two old men went arm-in-arm along the track. Sometimes one or other of them would give a bark of laughter or a cry of annoyance as his foot struck against a stone in the middle of the road.

The snow was falling thicker than ever. The old sailor passed his tobacco pouch to the old shepherd, but Sam had left his pipe at home. The match spurted, and the flame showed the hollowed cheeks of Ben as he drew in the smoke, before a falling snowflake fell on the burning match—a drifting moth—and quenched it.

It was the darkest night of winter, and such a snow cloud was drifting across the island that they couldn't see the lights of the village.

But they knew the general direction.

Once they both left the road and sallied against a barbed wire fence, and one of the travellers got a deep scrape on his hand, and a fencing post knocked the burning pipe out of the other's mouth.

Then they said one or two uncomplimentary things about the farmer who had been so inconsiderate as to put up his fence in that particular place. Ben found his pipe in the snow drift. Sam shook beads of blood from his hand.

They went on, grumbling and laughing.

'I hear trouble,' said the old shepherd.

'I hear nothing,' said the old skipper, 'but then I'm hard of hearing since that last trip I made to China.'

What came to them through the darkness was music—a fragment of a reel played on a fiddle—a scratching and a scraping that could only be made by Willie the miller.

'Well,' said Willie as the skipper and the shepherd came up to him where he stood at the buttress of the bridge over the burn, 'I thought I would be playing tonight to an owl and an otter maybe. But here come two old men. Imagine that.'

On the three old men walked together. And the snow fell thicker about them.

The miller put his trembling fiddle inside his coat.

The shepherd drew his scarf across his mouth.

There was a lighthouse miles away across the Pentland Firth, in Scotland. It pulsed regularly. The sky was clear to the south.

Sometimes one or other of them would say something, but the snow muffled the words. They struggled on, arm in arm, lifting heavy feet out of the drifted ruts.

Ben said, in the ringing voice he had once used on the quarter deck, 'I think we're in for a real blizzard. I feel it in my bones.'

It was as if his words put out the lighthouse. They could see its flashings no more. The night was thickening.

They stopped at the crown of the brae to get their breath.

'I'd have been better right enough,' said

the miller, 'playing this fiddle to the cat at home.'

In the slow wavering downward flake-drift their faces were three blurs.

'I'll tell you something,' said Ben. 'When I was in India a long while ago, I bought a piece of ivory from a merchant in Bombay. Well, I have a lot of interesting objects from all over the world at home. But this piece of ivory I always liked best. It has a bunch of grapes carved on it. Tonight I thought to myself, "Ben, what's the use of a houseful of treasures to an old man like you? You might be dead before the first daffodils in April." So I put the carving in my pocket and came out like an old fool into this blizzard.'

The three men stood there in the heart of the snowstorm.

'Well now,' said Sam the shepherd, 'that's a very strange thing you've said, Ben. I'll tell you why. I had three golden sovereigns put away in a stone jar on the mantelpiece. It had been there for twenty years. It was to pay for my funeral, that money. It struck me this afternoon at sunset—"They'll have to bury you anyway, Sam," I said to myself. "You're too old now to mind a pauper's grave. Why don't you take the money," said I to myself, "and give it to the living?"...'

The three old men laughed, a muffled

threefold merriment on the crown of the island.

The snow fell thicker still.

Willie the miller said, 'I tell you what—I've been working on a new fiddle tune since harvest. I think it's the best music I ever made. I call it *Milling the Barley*. I thought, "I'm going to play this reel somewhere where it'll be truly appreciated"... But where could that be?'

'We'd better be getting on then,' said Ben.

So they linked arms and put their heads into the slow black drift. Here and there the snow was up to their knees.

'Watch where you're going,' said Willie, as if the other two were responsible for their wayward progress.

Then they were all in a deep drift, topsy-turvy, a sprawl and a welter and struggle of old men!

They got to their feet, pulling at each other, shaking the snow off their coats, wheezing and grumbling.

'I tell you what,' said Ben, 'we've lost the road altogether. We'd best go carefully. We might be over the crag and into the sea before we know.'

They could hear, indeed, the surge and break of waves against the cliff, but whether near or far-off was hard to say, on such a night.

'We're lost, that's what it is,' said Sam.

Just then the snow cloud was riven, and in a deep purple chasm of sky a star shone out, and before the cloud closed in again they saw the farmhouse Skeld with a lamp in the window.

'We're on a true bearing,' said Ben the skipper. 'But what that star was I don't know.'

The snow was falling thicker than ever as they came to the first houses of the village.

Now they could hear the hullabaloo from the inn bar, shouts and mauled bits of song and the clash and clank of pewter, and the innkeeper calling, 'Less noise! I want no rows or fighting tonight. The policeman's on his way.'

The three were aware of a lantern near the end of the kirk, and when it was near enough the lantern light splashed the face of Tommy Angel, the boy who sometimes kept the inn fires going and washed the glasses and swept the inn floor.

'I was sent to meet you,' said Tommy, 'and take you to the place.'

They could have found their own way to the inn, with all that clamour and noise coming from the lighted door.

'Lead on, Tommy,' said Sam the shepherd.

The boy led them round the inn to the byre behind, where the innkeeper stabled his beasts in winter.

The old men could just see, through the veils of snow, the glim of a candle inside.

Ikey

JANUARY

There was once a tribe of tinkers in Orkney, who went from island to island selling clothespegs and tin mugs and bootlaces.

There was a boy called Ikey in this sprawling rootless family. Ikey liked to wander off by himself. He wasn't missed, there were so many laughing fighting sisters and brothers and cousins.

One stormy day in winter he came to a hut by the shore. An old woman opened to his tremulous whine. Ikey had the gift of joy and lamentation and everything in between. He could wear a score of masks. Ikey could see that the old woman in the cold empty hovel wouldn't live beyond the thaw. So Ikey took a few peats from the peatstack of a big farm nearby, and a few eggs from the henhouse, and a sheepskin from the shed, and a fistful of oats from the barn, and he brought them to the old woman... So they ate some porridge beside the fire, and Ikey told her a story that made her laugh. Then he went out into the new-fallen snow.

171

FEBRUARY

Ikey was in another island before the end of winter. He heard hushed voices in one croft-house. He looked through the window and saw a coffin with a long silver beard flowing half-way down it and the dead man had two pennies for eyes. Men and women stood here and there in the death room and they were passing a whisky bottle round and eating shortbread and cherry cake. They tried to keep their faces grave but sometimes their long faces curved and dimpled, and after a time, when the lamp was lit, a fiddler came in and there was much talk and laughter and—soon enough—dancing. Sometimes they would pause and say what a good person the dead crofter had been. Then a young woman saw Ikey's cold face squashed against the window, and she took him inside, and some of them said what a bonny boy he was (although ragged and dirty), and others said he should work hard and not beg and steal, and then he would have a good death like the dead man in his coffin, but the young woman gave him cheese and bannocks, and a thick slice of cake, and she even let him taste the hot sweet whisky... And she lit a lantern and took Ikey out to the straw of the barn to sleep.

MARCH

Sometimes the old tinker chief might say, 'Where's that boy Ikey? I haven't seen him for a week or two.' And a tinker wife would reply, 'Ikey's like the moon, he's here and gone again.' A tinker lass would say, 'Ikey's like a wave of the sea, he comes shining among us and then he's nothing but echoes and spray.'

The old chief said, 'Ikey is the tinker of tinkers. He's even an outcast from us vagrants. He's like the wind on the hill...'

The tinkers were camped in a quarry outside a village, but Ikey was in another part of that island, that March, where the big farms were. There was a ploughman in every field, and between every ploughman and his ox was a shining wavering furrow, and behind every wet clay furrow was a madhouse of wheeling gulls. Then at noon a servant woman came out to the ploughlands and left a jar of ale for every ploughman and a mouthful of hay for every ox. And the bones of the ploughmen creaked as they stretched themselves and the nostrils of the oxen seemed to belch

173

flame... But to one young ploughman came a pretty young woman, with a pot of ale in a pitcher, and she stirred sugar into the ale from a poke, and she gave the ploughman a pipe with new-rubbed tobacco in it, a few rum-smelling shreds spilling over the bowl and she lit the pipe and gave it to the ploughman. Then she kissed him, after he had taken a draw or two of burning tobacco.

The lass looked from time to time back at the big farm. The daughter of Steethe, that well-to-do farmer: there were other plans for Jane than to dally with a poor common farm labourer like Will Stout. Ikey thought he had never seen such a happy pair. Ikey knocked at the farm door and said to the grey-mouthed wife who stood there, 'You'll have a long life, lady, if you give me a sweet biscuit and a cup of tea...' The farm wife dreaded the threats and prophecies of the wandering ones, so she took Ikey into the kitchen and gave him a mug of strong tea and two caraway biscuits.

The farmer of Steethe was nodding half-asleep beside the fire. 'What about giving me a shilling?' said Ikey. 'You can well afford it. When Mr Rosey your man goes, you'll likely find a sack of sovereigns behind a loose stone in the byre...'

She gave Ikey a threepenny piece out

of her purse with shaking fingers. The old man nodded and sometimes gave a snore.

'My man has great worry with Jane our lass,' said she. 'We've promised her to Obadiah Richan of Skaillbreck, the wealthiest farmer in the whole parish, but the hussy won't speak to him. The worry has broken my man, it has put a grey whisker here and there on my chin too...'

'I can see your lass and what's to come of her,' said Ikey. 'That's fine mittens you have on your needles...'

So the wife hastened to knit the last few loops on the second mitten and she put them on Ikey's hands. (Ikey disliked gloves, and stockings too, but he knew the shopkeeper in the village was giving twopence-ha'penny for fleece-fresh gloves.)

'Happiness and joy and plenty she'll have, your lass,' said Ikey. 'And you'll have bonny grandbairns to greet over you when you die...'

The old farmer snored in his beard like an angry beehive.

'Here,' said the farm wife, 'take this pot of rhubarb jam.'

When Ikey left that farm the ploughman was half-way down a new furrow, and Jane the daughter of Steethe was crossing the stile as though every turning furrow was a page in the book of love.

But the nearer she got to the farm door, the more her steps began to drag.

APRIL

Miss Instone the teacher in Greenvoe village blew her whistle and all the island children—twenty of them—went swirling in through the door of the small school.

Ikey looked from the road outside.

Miss Instone took the whistle from her mouth and she said, 'You, boy, why aren't you at school? You're the age for school attendance, I know that... Why can't your mother clean you up, you're filthy! Why can't she put a stitch in your rags? Oh, you're a tinker boy, are you... Well, all the bairns in my school are neat and washed and shod, however poor they are... I don't want them getting fleas and lice... So you'd better not come in, not today... Still, realise this, you little wretch, you're breaking the law by not attending school. Your parents—if you have any—could be in serious trouble...'

Miss Instone went into the classroom and shut the door. 'Slates out!' she shouted. 'Spell the following words...'

On the hillside, a mile further on, Ikey sat on a stone. A little company of early daffodils, in bud still, hung their heads nearby. A small cloud moved over, scattering drops of rain. The green heads twinkled. Then there was a wash of sun across the hill.

A lark went up and up into the new patch of blue and was lost, but the sky went on ringing, it seemed even louder, over the hill of Greenvoe.

In the field above, a ewe called anxiously for her lamb, wandering here and there among the rocks and little marshes. (There had been much rain this April.) Then Ikey was aware of a small flutter beside him. It was a lamb like a tiny masker, all black with a white mask for eyes and white forelegs and a white tail. Ikey thought it strange that the very young have no fear, but soon the world is full of shapes of dread. The harlequin lamb nuzzled Ikey's knee. Ikey lifted it and carried it to the ewe.

The lark went on stammering out sweetness between two rain clouds.

Ikey was on the road, passing the small farm of Cleftbreck. He moved round Cleftbreck in a wide circle, because Rover the dog there had a bad reputation—indeed, once Rover had ripped a rag out of Ikey's trousers, and Ikey hadn't stopped running for a mile, his rags all a-flutter, his breath coming in sobs and gasps...

But Rover must have been out with Berston the farmer at the hill, for there was only Mistress Berston coming in from the henhouse with an aluminium bowl brimming over with eggs.

'Is that you, Ikey?' said the farm wife. 'Hold out your cap. I have more eggs than I know what to do with.'

Ikey held out his bonnet and Mistress Berston put six warm eggs into it, three brown and three white.

Ikey had never learned to say thank-you but his teeth flashed in his tinker face.

He hadn't eaten for two days. He broke an egg with his thumb and emptied it down his throat, then another...

The big cloud that had covered the sun ten minutes before dropped its rain, a lingering prismatic shower. Mistress Berston drew her shawl about her head and scurried indoors.

Ikey held his face up to the rain until his hair and his hands were streaming, and his hundred rags clung wetly about him. The sun came out again. Ikey glittered like a fish or a bird. The whole island was clean and sparkling.

Ikey broke another egg into his mouth. His throat wobbled.

Ikey ran back across the hill. More lambs had been born since he had sat on the stone at lark-rise.

As he looked, there was a faint stirring in the cluster of daffodil buds. Slowly, slowly, with a gesture of delight, the first daffodil opened in the wind.

MAY

The tinkers had moved to the island of Selskay at peat-cutting time—not that they would ever soil their hands toiling in the wet wounded bog; they preferred to beachcomb for driftwood. 'Good clean salt,' said the tinker chief. 'That peat smoke's bad for the lungs.'

The tinkers would blow up their fires of broken ship's timbers and simmer tin cans of rabbit stew at night, and tell stories that had been first told in fairs at Galway and Dingle three hundred years before.

Maybe, if there was a shortage of driftwood, they might 'take the loan' of a few peats from some abundant peat-stack in the depths of winter.

Ikey sat down at the edge of the Selskay peat-banks. There were half a hundred folk working in this bank and that. It was peat-cutting time in May. With a heavy squelch the spades sank into the wet bog, and the squares of turf were heaved on to the heather. And there they were set up in a hundred little dolmens for the winds

179

and suns of the long summer to dry.

At noon the peat-workers stopped and sat round in groups while the women went round with ale jars and big plates loaded with cheese and oat bannocks.

Ikey sat, as lonely as a kestrel, on the edge of this festival of labour.

A kind lass called Jessie-Ann swerved off from her round and went to Ikey and pushed oatcakes and cheese into Ikey's fists.

'You foolish slut!' cried a bearded farmer. 'This nourishment's for honest workers, not for the likes of them!' The man's voice was like a horn across the hill. The echoes sounded in the next valley. Jessie-Ann's ruddy face blanched. Ikey was startled too. He got up like a hare and bounded off in leaps across the hill. But he was clutching an oatcake and a wedge of cheese in one hand, and there was a fine blown lace of ale-froth across his cheek.

JUNE

The fishermen of Farn village were going down to their boat *Kestrel* one morning when whom should they meet but Merran with the black whisker.

No fisherman would dare put to sea,

having met Merran.

It was a promising fishing day. They sat on their boat and smoked and complained about witches and the evil eye.

'Look!' said Willie the famous creel-maker. 'Here's that tinker boy coming.'

Ikey was roaming here and there among the rockpools, looking for sea treasure, a salt-eaten boot or a broken oar.

'An innocent boy like Ikey might cancel a spell,' said Thorfinn, whose hooks were sharper and more barbed than any in Orkney.

Ikey refused to go out in the *Kestrel.* 'You don't have to do anything,' said the oldest fisherman, Jeemo. 'Just sit on the thwart and enjoy the sail.'

Ikey sat in the stern thwart. The sea got rough beyond Rousay, and Ikey leaned over the stern and spasms of sickness went through him.

But the lines came up burgeoning with haddocks, again and again. It was the best morning the Farn men had had fishing all that June. The five baskets amidship were over-brimming with fine fat haddocks.

At last they turned the *Kestrel* for home.

Ikey floundered ashore like a dying seal, grey in the face.

'The seasickness never killed anybody,' said the old skipper. 'You'll be as right as rain once you're on the shore road.'

There was a great feast of fish round the tinkers' fire that night.

Ikey's appetite was sharper than any seal's.

'I'm never going fishing again,' said Ikey, licking cod juice from his fingers. 'Never.'

JULY

There was a fine big merchant's shop in Hamnavoe kept by Mr James Corston, a magistrate and Justice of the Peace.

Mr Corston had made a fortune supplying the Hudson's Bay ships and the whaling ships; yet, as the townsfolk said, 'every penny was a prisoner' with Mr Corston.

If only Mrs Corston had been behind the counter, Ikey would have gone in. Mrs Corston frequently gave Ikey a paper poke of broken biscuits, whenever he passed through Hamnavoe. But, as the Hamnavoe folk said, old Corston 'wouldn't part with the dirt from under his fingernails'.

It was wearing on for the dinner hour. Mr Corston gravely consulted his gold watch. Then he locked up till two o'clock. 'Off with you,' he said to Ikey. 'I don't want the likes of you hanging about my shop door. Bad for trade.'

So Ikey wandered down fishing piers and up closes where housewives were digging up the first tatties of July.

Hamnavoe was full of cats, like all fishing towns.

Ikey was emerging from Garriock's Close on to the main street when a fist closed on his shoulder. 'You're coming along with me,' said Brunton the policeman. 'You young thief.'

And Ikey's feet hardly touched the cobblestones till he found himself in the single cell of the police station; then with a rasp and a screech the heavy iron key was turned in the lock.

Ikey could not imagine a more terrible place. His heart was pulsing inside him like a hen gathered up for the soup pot, or a hooked trout in the Harray Loch.

Brunton's face appeared at the grating. 'Now then, just tell me what you did with Bailie Corston's gold watch and you'll maybe get off with a few strokes of the birch rod. Speak up, you rag-bag.'

But Ikey couldn't say a word.

'This is a serious business,' said Brunton. 'Worst case I've known for years.'

The thunder cloud of his face disappeared, and the thunder of his voice.

Outside, it was a golden July day. There was nothing Ikey could do all afternoon but watch the square of sun moving along the wall. A blackbird visited the barred window of his cell and its glossy throat throbbed with song, twice. A honeybee blundered in and out.

Constable Brunton appeared with a hunk of bread and a mug of water. 'Better get used to this diet,' he said. 'I expect they'll put you away for twelve years for a serious crime like that...'

Ikey had been warned, round the quarry fire, to say nothing—not a word—to those in authority.

The bread stuck in his throat. He had tasted better water in the ditches.

A butterfly loitered in and lit on Ikey's hand and went out again into the wind and sun.

Ikey could hear the fishing-boats returning in the early evening. The air of his cell was heavy for a while with salt and herring smells.

The constable looked very grave when he clanged open the door and came in for Ikey's tin mug. 'Mr Corston's ill—doctor's been at him twice—worry about the theft of that gold watch—an heirloom, been in the Corston family four generations. Say Mr Corston died—say this dreadful crime was to be the end of him—then it might turn out to be a hanging matter, my lad. I would say my prayers, if I was you.'

Then the dreadful black clanging as

184

the cell door shut behind Brunton the policeman.

Ikey wondered where they would execute him. He had heard, round the quarry fires, that Gallowsha in Kirkwall was the place where witches and thieves were hanged. He imagined the immense crowd there would be under the gallows. There used to be a lot of drinking and dancing on the days of an execution. He wondered if the tinkers would be there, with Benjie his cousin playing a lament on the bagpipe... Oh, no, the whole tribe would scatter through Caithness or Shetland—anywhere to be away from the disgrace.

Ikey tried to comfort himself. Butterflies die, bees die, blackbirds die. It's the way of nature. Night comes, the lantern is snuffed out, there is blackness and silence. It happens to all sun-loving creatures. But to die that way, the centre of a mocking screeching dancing mob, and innocent, and alone—that was too horrible!

Constable Brunton's key screeched in the lock.

The square of sun had just faded from the high corner of the cell, and the first shadows were gathering. 'Have they come for me already?' thought Ikey...

Brunton said, 'All right you, get out. And a good riddance.'

Within a minute Ikey was standing

185

outside in the street, shivering, with tears of joy on his face. And there, on the far side of the street, stood Mrs Corston. 'You poor boy,' she said. 'Come home with me now and have a bite of supper. It's all been a terrible mistake.'

'Is Mr Corston dead?' said Ikey. 'Why aren't you wearing a black shawl?'

'Him dead!' she cried. 'He's too miserable to die. The thought of the funeral expenses will keep him alive till he's the age of Methuselah. So long as there's a penny profit to be made he'll hang on. Die, indeed! Corston's too mean to have dealings with doctors and undertakers.'

'Well,' said Ikey, 'it wasn't me stole his gold watch.'

'The old fool put it in the pigeon-hole beside his ledger, at dinnertime. And then he forgot where he'd put it. I never saw such rage and such panic! The last face he saw was the tinker boy in his doorway. So it must have been you.'

Soon Ikey was sitting at the Corston's kitchen table, eating a great wedge of Mrs Corston's ginger cake and drinking ginger beer out of a good china cup.

There was a shuffling outside the kitchen door, and a few throat-clearings, and there stood Bailie Corston hesitating on the threshold.

'I wondered how long it would be till

you came to apologise to the boy,' said Mrs Corston. 'Better late than never.'

Two strides took the shopkeeper to Ikey's side. He opened his white-knuckled fist and set a coin on the table beside Ikey's cup. It was new mint crown, a five shilling piece.

Then Mr Corston turned and blundered out again, without a word.

'Well,' said Mrs Corston. 'To think of that! It must be like tearing his heart out by the roots.'

Ikey slept that night in the barn of Glebe, among straw, the richest boy in the world.

AUGUST

Something wonderful happened every August, in the town of Kirkwall, in the shadow of St Magnus Cathedral—the Lammas Fair.

From Scotland came the travelling fairground people—the Orcadians called them 'the play-actors'. The play-actors set up their booths on the market green, between the main street and the great red minster that had stood there for seven hundred years and more.

There was a one-eyed man with a barrow of coconuts.

There was the lady with the fishtail.

There was the dwarf with the monkey and the barrel-organ.

There was the cheapjack who sold watches, price one shilling, that went for twenty-four hours or thirty-six hours and then were silent forever; but the cheapjack uttered cajolery and mockery in a non-stop flood that it was better than any ballad, just to listen to him. (And of course he had shaken the dust of Kirkwall from his feet by the time the dud watches ceased their ticking...)

There was a turbaned dark man from Afghanistan who sold coloured silk scarves and cushion covers from an open sandal-wood case.

There was the strong man in the tiger skin who could lift four great ploughmen in the air at one time, they standing on a wooden board across his chest.

There was the knife-thrower who threw knives all round a beautiful girl, and she smiling as the knives went quivering into a wooden frame—an inch wrong and she would have been transfixed like a butterfly in a case.

There was the fortuneteller whose face was veiled, inside a tent full of whispers and promises and dooms, and the shadow of silver on her hand. Country lasses came out, all giggles and flusters.

188

There were beer tents and lemonade tents and tents reeking blue with fried bloody puddings and boiled mussels.

There was even, that August, an Italian with a fine curling waxed moustache who sold ice-cream—a thing not known in Orkney before.

There was, as there seemed to have been from time's beginning, a blind fiddler who moved through the throngs of townsfolk and country folk.

Ikey was there the day the three magistrates arrived with a scroll and ordered the play-actors to leave the cathedral forthwith and never sully the kirk green again. The city herald beat on his drum and the tumultuous noises of the Lammas Fair died away. Then the herald led the three city magistrates away.

They had hardly gone back into the town hall when the fairground began its circlings and laughter and cajolings and music and dancing and feasting again. The noise and bustle increased as the day went on.

Ikey's tattered cap was quite heavy with pence and half-pence. A tipsy sailor had even thrown in a sixpence.

The magistrates appeared again, very grave and stern, the provost carrying the scroll. The herald beat on his drum, thrice, but its throbs were lost in the huge

Lammas tumult. And all that could be seen of the provost's proclamation was his mouth opening and shutting like a fish.

Ikey's lips were purple with the crumbs of a big bloody pudding. The ice-cream throbbed in his throat with delicious dollops. His bonnet was overspilling with copper coins. He had never known a Lammas Fair the like of this.

Suddenly, just at sunset, the great west door of St Magnus opened and the minister appeared.

The fair ground to a halt, hushed into silence, at sight of the good old man standing on the steps of the kirk.

'Good folk,' he said, 'this fair has gone on here, in this very place, for hundreds of years. It is Lammas, the time of the ripening of corn so that we may all eat and drink next winter—a day for rejoicing surely. There are people, important people, men in authority, who would turn every sweet and joyful ceremony into sourness. It may be that soon they will prevail, for their voices grow stronger in the land with every passing year. It may be, there will be no Lammas Fair in the shadow of St Magnus, soon. Make merry and rejoice, good people, for another summer has crowned our labours with fruitfulness.'

After a moment of silence, a mighty cheer went up from the Lammas revellers.

By the light of the first flares, Ikey set out to find his people in the dense surging throngs. He had bought 'fairings' for them all: little pokes of sweeties, scotch mixture and cinnamon drops and butternuts and claggam and pan-drops and mints so clear you could see through them, like glass.

But his folk had gone away under the first stars.

SEPTEMBER

It was September, the harvest month.

Everybody that could glean or bind a stook, even children and cripples and old men who had sat all summer in the chimney corner, were called out to the oat-field, when the wind filled the crop with heaving burnish; for who knew when wind and rain might come together and ruin all the rich promise of summer...

Ikey wandered to the quarry one morning in early September to find it empty of tents. The tribe had moved on to some island where there was only fishing and fowling—Foula, maybe, or Auskerry, or Rona.

'You, boy,' said a no-nonsense voice behind him, 'what are you idling here for? Everybody's in the laird's field cutting the barley...' It was Snoddy, Sir Thomas's factor. 'Follow me. I'll find a job for you.'

Ikey followed Mr Snoddy as far as the crossroads, then he lay down in a ditch until the factor, an urgent man that day, disappeared over the ridge. Snoddy saw disaster in every cloud, in every stir of air. A sudden storm would ruin everything!

Ikey knew in his bones that there would be no rain or gales for a week at least. (All his people could read the weather: they felt snow in their marrow a week before a blizzard—they sensed the stir and throb of grass seeds under the blackest frost...)

Work in the laird's barley-field under the bitter eye and tongue of Snoddy!...Ikey laughed at the idea.

Still, he liked to watch the harvesters at their burnished labour, under the mild September sun—the striding swinging scythemen, the women gathering sheaves and setting up stooks, the children (free from school for a fortnight) chasing the rabbits who were bolting this way and that from their narrowing kingdom of barley.

And there stood Snoddy at the edge of the field, shouting every half-hour or so that a storm was breeding out there in the Atlantic—they must hurry, hurry! The last corn must be cut before sunset.

The crofters, if they paid any attention to Snoddy at all, looked at him with mild contempt. They had their own harvests to cut, after the laird's crop was gathered in... The men would hone their scythes and spit on their hands from time to time, and once more wade thigh-deep among the scythed susurrant stalks.

Ikey only showed himself at midday, when the harvesters leaned against the stooks and the women and girls went among them with cheese and oatcakes and ale. Snoddy had gone up to his cottage beside the laird's big house. He would never demean himself by eating with the common crofters.

Ikey squatted next to a happy young couple. He hadn't seen such joyful faces all year, not even at the Lammas Fair. At once he recognised the young man who had ploughed that field in March and the lass from the farm who had gone to meet him at the end of a furrow, with such tremulous happiness on her face, and then returned to her sour parents, all hesitant guilt and foreboding...

Now they sat by themselves, a little apart from the other harvesters, as happy as though the whole golden field belonged to them, and all the other uncut fields of Orkney too... They were so engrossed in each other, that pair, that all the harvesting islanders might have been kindly bronze shadows, coming and going around them.

Snoddy returned, and the women packed the remnants of the meal into baskets, and the men knocked the embers out of their pipes. Will Stout the farm labourer and Jane Rosey of Steethe farm sat on, in their trance of happiness.

Snoddy shouted at them, 'Going to be wed next month, I hear. Well, it'll be a poor hungry hearth you'll keep unless you work a bit harder than you've worked today!'

Jane and Will Stout got to their feet. They even put glad looks on Snoddy.

Then Jane Rosey noticed Ikey trying to hide behind a stook from the factor. 'Ikey,' she said, 'you can come to our wedding too.'

Will and Jane went down among the shimmering barley and the flashing scythes, hand in hand.

Ikey was rummaging in baskets of leftovers, a chicken-bone and a few crusts, when he noticed a very old man wiping silver drops from his beard with a red-spotted bandana. The old man was too feeble for work. It was tears, not sweat, that he was wiping away—that the daughter of the ancient farm of Steethe should be marrying a common ploughman...

Ikey didn't go to the wedding in the barn of Steethe farm.

What would the wedding guests have said if he had turned up in his rags, smelling of ditch fires and mussels from the ebb?

Still, he did splash water in his face out of the burn. The island springs and waterfalls overflowed all the month of October; for no sooner was harvest in, in the last poorest bleakest croft among the heather, then the rain fell in spates and tumults, and still great herds of grey-black clouds came stampeding out of the Atlantic, day after day, with sodden splashing hooves.

There was an hour of watery sun for the wedding procession, as it wound back from the manse to the festive barn of Steethe. First the fiddler, then bridegroom and bride, groomsman and bridesmaid, and the wedding guests in their best clothes (the men in white shirts and dark suits, the women in shawls and bright new dresses); and the parish boys shouting in the barn yard, as the procession arrived, for money to buy a wedding football.

The procession was met at the barn door by the bride's father.

Ikey saw from the end of the road how grave and dignified the old man was, now that the kirk had blessed the marriage, and he accepted that, though his name would die out, his blood would certainly flow on through many generations.

And so the old farmer welcomed them all into the barn where his wife and a score of women were laying out the wedding dinner. The air was rich with the smell of whisky and new ale and Jamaican sugar and spices: a man with a face as red and round as a harvest moon was preparing the bride-cog, a drink of wondrous joy or wretched after-woe, according to the sagacity of the drinker, as the brimming portable barrel went round and round in sunward circles all evening, till well beyond midnight.

Ikey lingered for an hour beside the stye. The stars pierced him like nails. Hunger gnawed in his belly like a wolf—for the wedding supper was in full swing, and soon, once the brothpot and the stewpot had been borne away, the fiddler would be king of the revels.

Ikey was just turning to go back to the cold quarry when a white shadow glided in front of him. The shadow smelt too fragrant for a ghost, and no ghost ever spoke so sweetly and happily at midnight.

'I'm glad you've come, Ikey,' said the bride. 'It means we'll have a long happy life, Will Stout and I. You must wet your mouth with the bride-cog.'

She handed the rich-fuming tub to Ikey. And Ikey was so cold he took a long deep draught from it, and then another, and another.

The bride kissed him on his new-washed cheek.

'The bride, the bride!' they were calling from the lighted lurching barn. 'Where's the bride? It's time for the wedding march.'

Music flashed from the fiddler's bow.

The bride crossed the barnyard to the barn like a drift of moonlight between two clouds.

Ikey didn't remember how he got home to the quarry that night—his going was half a dance and half a stagger, with a rest now and then in a wet ditch. But it was a journey of great happiness—whether from that hot sweet concoction in the cog or from the kiss he had gotten from the bride, Ikey couldn't say.

When he woke next morning beside the hot stone, the tribe had moved in to another island. He was alone.

More rain had fallen in the night. His coat was sodden. He quenched his raging thirst from a pool in the quarry.

His head ached but his heart still glowed like the last embers in the tinkers' fire.

Everybody knew that Sir Thomas Damsay the laird hadn't been keeping too well.

'Too much brandy and oysters and roasted grouse,' said Swart the blacksmith.

The laird had had to leave Parliament in mid-session and come home.

'You'd have thought,' said Tommy the ferryman, 'if there was all that much wrong with him, he'd be better off with grand specialist doctors in London than with old Logan.' (Dr Aeneas Giles Logan had qualified in medicine in Glasgow half a century before, and he generally advised patients that Nature would cure them if only they waited long enough.)

'I can set a broken limb, or pump seawater out of a half-drowned man,' he would say. 'Nature does the rest.' He kept a few bottles of coloured water in his surgery to keep some of the women quiet, who were always complaining... He spent his winters reading the Latin poets, Horace and Virgil, and his summers on the trout loch.

He could be very ill-natured if he got summoned in the middle of the night to a confinement or a sick-bed... 'Nature,' he would grumble, mounting his horse, and taking a swig from his pewter flask. 'They come and they go. Nature sees to it all. What do they want to disturb a harmless old man like me for?'... But, once arrived at the house of pain, nobody could be kinder and more comforting. His withered hands remembered the skills of half a century before, that had won him a *magna cum laude* degree at the medical school in Glasgow...

Dr Aeneas Logan visited the patient twice a day.

Swart the blacksmith always said, 'The man that whisky inside and Archangel tar outside won't cure would be better dead.'

Madge Holm from the shore said that water from the ancient well near her house would cure any disease. It had had a saint's name, once, that well, but over the centuries the islanders had forgotten it. But still, furtively, a bucket of that medieval healing water was brought to somebody bedridden with arthritis or the black wasting cough.

'Sir Thomas is a bit off colour,' Snoddy would say to anyone who dared to ask. 'None of your business anyway. He'll be up and about at the weekend...'

One morning the island woke to find the flag flying at half mast over the Hall... 'Nature,' said Dr Logan to the ferryman at the pier. 'We wither like leaves on the tree. Best to get blown down in a sudden gust. Comes to us all...'

Lady Damsay who had been a quiet woman all her days, began to busy herself about the ceremony of death.

November, she knew, was the month of the dead.

The body of Sir Thomas was laid out in the dining hall, with six candles burning. The important people of the island were invited to pay their respects before the interment. Teaston the merchant, Revd Mr McAlpine the minister (though the laird was to be buried according to Episcopalian rites), Andrew Coubister who had Bu, the largest farm in the island, the Provost of Kirkwall, the Lord Lieutenant, the six Commissioners of Supply, the lairds of Norday, Hellya and St Michael parish, Captain Fergus of the Leith passenger ship *Creggan*.

Mr Snoddy sorted all this better class of person in rough order of precedence, in the waiting room. The crofters and fishermen didn't get farther than the gate.

Lady Damsay received them, one after the other, at the door leading to the 'vasty hall of death'... Lady Damsay had always seemed to those mourners an anxious careworn flustered woman. This afternoon she seemed tranquil and beautiful.

One by one the mourners stepped into the wavering pool of candlelight, looked briefly into the stony coffined face, then passed on into the shadows beyond.

The reverent silence was broken by a harsh whisper of Snoddy in the great doorway, 'You trash! You scarecrow! I'll thrash you within an inch of your life. The insolence! Back with you to the quarry, you ragbag!'...

Lady Damsay hurried outside, and said a few tranquil words.

She returned with Ikey, and set him midway in the procession, between the Provost of Kirkwall and Captain Fergus. The boy smelt of grass fires and mussel shells.

He stood on tiptoe to look down into the cold face. The only thing Ikey remembered of the religion of his Irish ancestors (his great-great-grandfather had been a laird in Killarney, an aristocrat, exiled from his house and lands by some upstart colonel in Cromwell's army of occupation) was that in moments of solemnity or joy or thankfulness a person made the sign of the cross. This Ikey did, and stumbled down the step into the shadows where the long lugubrious faces glimmered.

When the last silent tribute had been paid, and Sam Johnston the joiner was hammering the first nail in the coffin, and Snoddy was pouring out his best Old Orkney malt from a crystal decanter, Lady Damsay said, 'Ikey, I'm specially pleased that you've come today... You must visit me again.'

Thud—thud—thud, went the nails in the coffin.

Ikey crossed the fields with a sack of funeral meats and bread over his shoulder, after the solemn funeral in the family vault.

He met Dr Logan coming up from the shore, reading an old book.

'Nature,' said Dr Logan. 'We all come out of wind, water, stone, fire. We get shaken back into them in the end. A good thing, eh, boy? I've been reading this Greek poet called Sophocles. He cheers me up always, that old poet. It's best, he says, never to be born at all. Next best is to go back into the elements as soon as Nature says the word, the sooner the better. He's by with it now, Sir Thomas. I don't have that much longer to go myself. You look happy enough, boy. I think Nature'll hang on to you for a good while yet...I didn't go to the funeral. Can't abide all them long faces.'

'May he rest in peace,' said Ikey.

Dr Logan opened his book and passed on, his mouth moving silently, savouring every syllable.

DECEMBER

That midwinter, Ikey looked everywhere in the islands for his people.

It was a cold December.

There were houses where he could have got food and a fire, and maybe a cast-off coat, and a strewment of straw to sleep on.

He could have knocked at the door of the Hall—that is, if Snoddy didn't see him first—and Lady Damsay would have been kind to him.

There would be a welcome at Steethe too, from Janet and Will and the grumpy old man.

But Ikey wanted to sit at the fire in the quarry with his people and listen to his grandmother tell the stories of the great rich people they had been, long ago in Ireland, until Cromwell's soldiers came with their muskets and torches, and drove them out on to the roads for ever. It was a grand thing to hear, the lamentation old Bridie could put into her tales.

Ikey's grandfather would say then, 'Ah, there's poorer folk in the world than us. We should be thankful.'

Nobody knew anything about the tinkers that winter, in Kirkwall or in Hamnavoe or in any village or island.

A fisherman set Ikey ashore after sunset

in a very lonely island.

The stars were sharp as thorns.

Once there had been five crofts in this island, and even a kirk and an alehouse, but the last family had left twelve winters before.

Ikey had seen, from the far shore, a lantern in one of the ruins. He was sure his people were there, taking baked potatoes out of a fire of peat and driftwood, drinking tea, telling the old stories of noble lineage...Ikey had mentioned it to the fisherman, who was just pushing out to lift his creels before the storm came. 'A lantern?' the fisherman had said. 'I don't see any light.'

Still, he had taken Ikey across the sound and set him on the deserted shore.

Soon Ikey knew that he should have stayed where he was, for there was no sound of songs or stories or argument. And the lantern was no longer there.

Then the wind got up and brought the first whirl of snow.

Ikey looked for a lee wall to spend the night. He didn't know when he might get back again to the big island of horses and fires.

The blizzard passed, the wind freshened, the stars tore his face like thorns.

Ikey stood in the ruin that had once been the alehouse. There was a shed in the yard. Like enough it had been a byre when the island was a little tumult of people a hundred years ago, at harvests and peat-cuttings.

A light shone through a chink of the stone wall.

How cold it must be for those strangers, whoever they were! Ikey broke a window frame over his knee, to take for kindling to the hidden soft song of the woman and the hidden sweet cry of the child.

A Nativity Tale

'I like this time of year,' said Gerston of the village inn, 'icicles, storms, and all.'

Thomasina puts whisky in a pot on the stove till it begins to chuckle. Then she pours it in a jug and mixes in sugar, just when the fishermen come up from the shore with snowflakes in their beards.

Thomasina Gerston shovelled the last of the snow away from the inn yard.

There in a corner of the cabbage patch she spied a cluster of snowdrops.

'Yes,' said Thomasina to Robbie Seatter the farm worker at the Glebe. 'If you wait long enough, spring always comes... It's no use asking Gerston for a mug of ale, Robbie, if you have no twopence... Maybe if you offered to plough Gerston's small field next month.'

'Well, ox,' said Robbie Seatter to the ox in the inn byre, 'you've had a good winter, ox, with a thatch over your head and hay and turnips.

'Now you must do some work. You see

this yoke. Take a good took at Gerston's old plough.

'The sun'll be glad to see us, ox, and the seagulls.

'I'm to get a bottle of whisky from the skinflint, ox, when the field's all ploughed.'

'No end of labour,' said Gerston's ox. 'That ploughing nearly killed me. I thought I was due a rest,' said the ox to Jenny the inn-lass. 'Nothing doing, I had to drag harrows two days, after all that.

'Tomorrow's Easter,' said the ox to Jenny who made butter and cheese for the inn.

'What's Ben the ox grumbling about?' said Jenny as on she went to the two cows whose breath smelt of new grass.

May morning, and the hill Kringfea sparkling. There on the summit Jenny of the inn and half a dozen other lasses wash their face in the May dew.

Old Margaret-Ann goes inn-ward with an empty pewter flask hidden under her shawl.

'Once I was bonnier than any of them,' said Margaret-Ann. 'Sorrow and sea-loss and farm labour will make scarecrows of them, let them wait... Put a gill of rum in this flask,' said the old woman to Gerston. 'I have a bad cough on me. Time enough to die in the winter.'

The island lasses went past the inn door. Their faces shone like daffodils.

One by one, the daffodils began to shrivel in the stone jam jar in Margaret-Ann's window.

It was midsummer, Johnsmas, in the island.

Margaret-Ann sat outside her door in the sun, turning her wheel, and drew out a fine grey line of wool from the fleece of Maimie the sheep.

A stranger in a black coat came up from the inn. He said to the old woman, 'I've come to have a look at you. I'll see you again in winter, to settle accounts with you.'

Margaret-Ann's wheel stopped turning.

The tall man in the black coat went down to the ferry-boat and sailed away.

'No,' said Gerston the innkeeper, 'there was no man in a black coat in this inn today.'

And 'No,' said Thorfinn the ferryman, 'I ferried no man in a black coat across the Sound today.'

The lark over Kringfea sang the sun down into the ocean, late, late.

The fine tourists came in the ferry-boat day after day, with binoculars, seeking the hen harrier and golden eagle and seals. They drank ale and ate cheese and oatcakes in the inn, and returned on the ferry in the long lingering light.

Finer tourists came with guns to shoot grouse and with rods to catch loch trout. They stayed at the inn.

Gerston was all unction and servility to the gentlemen.

And they slept in the three bedrooms, that Jenny had sweetened with tall lupins, and with marigolds from the marsh, and with meadowsweet.

The grouse hung from an inn rafter, the twelve trout lay in a great blue dish on the inn dresser.

The corn grew tall and green in the island fields.

Robbie Seatter, weary with the gold dust and silver sweat of harvest, laid his blunt scythe against the barn wall of Glebe farm.

The island was covered with stooks like an army besieging the Fortress of Hunger.

This harvester was too weary even to drink at the inn.

The shadow of Gerston stood at the barn door.

'I want my small field cut before sunset,' said Gerston.

'You owe two pounds five shillings and twopence for beer,' said Gerston. 'I'll forget about that.'

So Robbie Seatter honed his scythe and went down and cut Gerston's oat-field, and he bound the last sheaf before midnight.

Then the harvester washed the corn dust from his throat with a quart mug of ale.

The horseman sat secretly by the light of a lantern in the biggest barn in the island, and went through their ceremony.

They praised the horse, noblest of animals.

They praised the work of the blacksmith who forges steel shoes for the horse.

They praised the saddler for the well-made horse collar, and saddle and bridle and bit.

They praised the wind, brother of the swift horse.

They praised the waves of the sea, the salt spumy sisters of the horse.

They praised the ploughman, first friend of the horse. They praised the sower, next friend of the horse. They praised the merry scarecrow. They praised the scythemen and the women who bind sheaves. They praised the gatherers into barns, the flailers, the winnowers, the mill and the miller, the kneader of the dough and the hearth-baker and the steeper of malt for ale.

They praised all the servants of the horse.

Then (alas) they discovered that, though they had the loaf of bread on the trestle, they had forgotten the crown of the ceremony: the bottle of whisky.

Then Robbie Seatter was sent down to the inn with a half-crown, at midnight, to buy a bottle of Old Orkney malt.

There lay old Margaret-Ann in her coffin early in November, the month of the dead.

The croft women stirred about the house to see that all things were done in order.

And the very oldest woman in the island, who never slept, said she had seen the night before a man in a long black coat carrying a lantern, and the man had knocked on Margaret-Ann's door. And Margaret-Ann had opened the door to him.

The women went on preparing the funeral feast, cheese and oatcakes and ale.

Sam the undertaker came and he nailed the lid on the coffin.

A few of the women wept.

The very oldest woman said quietly, 'It won't be that long till the long dark man with the lantern comes knocking on my door.'

Then the six neighbour men came in to carry the coffin to the kirkyard where the minister was waiting with his book, and the gravedigger with his spade.

Then Jenny came from the inn with a bottle of whisky for the mourners to drink afterwards: a gift from Mr Gerston.

'Wonders will never cease,' said the woman from the neighbouring croft.

The very oldest woman said to Jenny from the inn, 'The grass withereth, the flower fadeth.'

Night fell. They lit a lamp. The women heard a shuffling of feet on the brig stones outside the door: the men back from the kirkyard.

Very important people came with the first snow: the sheriff officer and his clerk and three officials. Five crofters were so behind with their rent that the laird had decided to evict them. Out the defaulters must go, bag and baggage, snow or no snow.

It had been a poor harvest, after all.

The sheriff officer and his men stayed at the inn.

The snow fell thicker.

It was such a night that only a half-dozen crofters and fishermen stood at the bar. Thomasina Gerston poured hot water into their rum, and spooned in sugar.

The wind began to howl outside, and the

snow thickened and came horizontally and drifted the ditches and the island hollows under.

The important officials finished their supper at the inn fire and went upstairs to bed.

Then there was a knock at the door.

Ben the ox in the byre stopped munching hay and listened.

Presently the byre door opened and Gerston stood there with a lantern.

'You can bide here,' he was saying. 'Move over, Ben.'

Dancey

A boy, William Ness of the croft of Eard, was on the hillside one day, walking into the tail of a blizzard, well muffled, to see if any of his father's sheep was in trouble, when he saw someone approaching slowly, rising and falling in the drifts.

The blizzard had moved on southwards, and now the sky was clearing over the islands. William Ness saw that the stumbling lost one was a woman. He had never seen her before. He approached, cautiously.

The boy asked her who she was, and where she was going. She only shook her head.

She was wearing a grey cloak with a hood, and it was soaked, more coldly and intensely than any hour-long blizzard could have penetrated. Her coat hung so heavy on her that she could hardly stand, much less walk.

After his faltering questions had got no answer, his first impulse was to turn and run home as fast as he could. Women from the sea still moved through the old men's winter stories, and that and a hundred

214

other images were vivid and terrifying and beautiful in the boy's mind.

The young woman turned and pointed back towards the cliff and the open sea, whose cold blue brightness was beginning to be blurred and stained by another blizzard. Then, more insistently, she pointed to the sheep shelter further up the hill. She laid her cold wet hands on the boy, and she said over and over again, urgently, a single syllable that he could not understand. Her whole body yearned towards the sheepfold, over which the first snowflakes of the oncoming blizzard were now drifting.

William Ness shook his head. Words were useless. He pointed towards the valley below and the seven or eight crofts with smoke rising from the chimneys. There they might be able to help her. There were a few old sailormen in the valley. Perhaps they would understand her tongue.

She consented, with a weary shake of the head, to go with him. Meantime the entire sound, and the coast beyond, were blotted out by the snow cloud. Flakes swirled thickly round the woman and the boy. A lamp had been lit in the croft of Eard. It dimmed in the storm's onset. The further crofts were ghost houses.

The nearness of help and warmth seemed to give the young woman new strength. She

215

walked alongside him. He could smell the strong salt from her clothes. Once or twice she stumbled on a rock or in a rut. The boy was familiar with the ground. He held out his hand to her. The intense coldness of her clutch put a shudder through his body that reached as far as his heart. But he held on tight and led her down a sheep path.

Near a spring where some of the higher valley crofts got their water the stranger stopped. She bent down and kissed the boy. Then her knees gave and she collapsed.

'Come on!' said William Ness, shaking her. 'We're nearly there.'

She did not stir. He touched her face. His fingers flinched away from a still more bitter coldness. He turned and ran helter-skelter through the thickening blizzard to his parents' croft.

The room was full of neighbours. It was one of the last days of Yule, when the families trooped from croft to croft with little gifts.

William brought into the house a swirl of flakes. The flame in the lamp leapt in the draught.

'Shut the door, boy,' said his father.

'You're that cold!' cried his mother. 'Come over and sit by the fire.'

The stout brisk woman from the next croft, Madge, chafed his hands till the bones ached.

A fisherman put a whisky glass to his mouth and bade him drink. A fine fire kindled in his stomach and comforted all his body. Two or three valley children came about him. They imitated this old one and that. They plucked mimicry and laughter from each other. William laughed too.

His mother carried round a board of cheese and oatcakes. His father followed with the huge crock of ale.

Billo who had been a sailor began to sing a ballad but forgot the words. They rallied him with mockery and encouragement. He tried again, twice, and faltered. At last they latched his mouth with a glass of whisky. There was much laughter.

The door opened. The laird's gardener came in. They saw that the night was thick with stars. The newcomer opened his whisky bottle...

One by one the children began to yawn and rub their eyes. Two of them curled up in a corner beside the uneasy dog and went to sleep.

In a lull of the conversation, William said, 'I met a strange woman on the hillside. She fell down. She's still out there. Maybe we should go out and bring her in.'

But William had such a low voice that only his mother and Madge heard him.

'I declare', said his mother, 'that boy sees things that nobody else sees.'

'A bairn's imagination,' said Madge. 'They grow out of it.'

Then Tommy the joiner, after much pleading, put his fiddle to his chin and began to play. Pair by pair the young folk circled each other in the middle of the floor. The old man Anders stuck a red-hot poker in his mug till the ale hissed and steamed; as if he didn't have enough of a flame in his face already.

Round and round the dance went. William drowsed with his head on Madge's great stony knee.

Near midnight the door was thrown open. The newcomer was so coated in snow they did not recognise him until he had wiped the grey mask off his face. The music stopped. The dance faltered and stilled. It was Mr Spence, the general merchant from the north side of the island, five miles away. 'A good Yule to you all,' he said gravely.

'You're welcome,' said William's mother. 'We didn't expect a visitor from so far away on such a night.'

'I came to say, a ship struck on the reef of Hellyan in the snow storm this afternoon, just before sunset. The shore's covered with bodies. They've all been taken into the kirk hall. Tommy Wilson,

218

I came specially to see you, about coffins. Thirty-two bodies so far. The minister and the schoolmaster think she might have been an emigrant ship, out of the Baltic bound for America. There were a dozen women, most of them young. There were half a dozen bairns, God help them.'

William's father poured out a large dram for the newsbearer. Some of the whisky splashed on to the table.

There would be no more music or dancing that night...

There was silence. Then a small pure voice repeated his story of the young foreign woman on the hill. 'She's still there,' said William Ness. 'She fell and wouldn't get up again.'

His father raged at him, 'Why didn't you tell us this?' William hid his face in Madge's skirts.

Three young men were putting on their coats and caps. A lantern was brought from the cupboard and lit.

'Thirty-three coffins,' said Tommy. 'I'll have to send to Hamnavoe for wood.'

'There'll be wood in plenty from the ship,' said the factor. 'Staves and planks everywhere. They'll take their ship with them under the earth.'

'She fell beside the spring,' whispered William.

The searchers, going out, paused. 'Beside

the spring...' There had been so much snow all night that if a woman were lying near the spring she would have the whole hillside for her shroud. They knew every contour; they must look for a long low hump.

The pure sweet voice of the boy spoke again. 'The sheepfold,' William said. 'Look there, too. The woman kept pointing at the sheepfold.'

An hour later, two of the searchers brought in the body of the young woman and laid it in the barn.

The third man returned half an hour later, carrying a child. It was still alive. The peat basket was emptied of peats, and blankets were laid in it and the child was set in a nest of blankets.

A spoonful of watered whisky was tilted into the infant's mouth. The child opened its eyes and cried once—a sound new but older than all languages—then it drifted into sleep beside the hearth.

What should be done with it?

'There's bairns in every croft in this valley, but mine,' said Madge. 'I'll take it, if nobody else wants it. I'll have the blessing of a bairn without the burden of a man.'

Nobody disputed the fostering.

Well after midnight Madge Selquoy carried the shipwrecked child to her croft across a field deep and blue-black under snow.

It looked like being a good harvest in the valley, nurtured all summer with bounteous sun and a sufficiency of rain.

A generation had passed since the shipwreck. A slow wave of time had gone over the valley, taking away some old ones (and also, as sometimes happens, a few young fishermen were scattered and lost in a quick wave of the sea). But always there was a stirring of children in this croft or that: the rise and fall of generations.

Particularly in the croft of Strom down at the shore there was rarely silence while the sun was up. The solid rooftree was shaken morning to night with cajolery, laughter, hectoring, rage, songs. The woman of the house, Dancey, had been ten years married to Andrew Crag who had the fishing boat *Hopeful*. They also had a few acres where they kept two cows and grew potatoes and cabbages and oats, and they had a score of sheep on the hill. But most of what nourished Andrew and Dancey Crag and their six children came out of the sea.

And Dancey would help push the boat *Hopeful*, loaded with creels or lines, into the sea in the morning, up to her thighs in the cold water. And then again, in the afternoon or early evening Dancey was there when *Hopeful* returned, sometimes heavy with fish, sometimes with only a thin scattering along the bottom boards.

'What are you thinking about?' she would say tartly to Andrew whenever there was a poor catch. 'How am I going to feed your bairns on a few trashy haddocks like this?'

Andrew would remark mildly that he had no control over the vagrancies of fish. 'I do my best but I can't compel them.'

Plenitude or scarcity, Dancey would take the basket of fish on her back and hump it up to Strom, where several mewling cats waited for her, and gulls flashed above waiting for the gutting to begin.

Inside, the youngest child might be wailing from its crib, and two little ones playing with water or wild flowers on the doorstep; the three eldest were safely folded in the school. Many a morning, that fine summer, while Dancey made butter or stoked the hearth for the baking of bannocks, she could hear the murmurs of multiplication, poetry, geography, drifting from the small school above.

'A few poor things of mackerel,' she said to Andrew one day. 'Go up to the hill, see if the sheep are all right. I think you might be better with sheep than fish. If the weather holds, there might be a good harvest. There'd better be.'

Then she turned and gave the five-year-old boy Joe a ringing slap on the side of his head for putting his fingers in the butter. And Joe yelled as if the sky had fallen down on him. And Andrew went away up to the hill to see to the sheep.

Even in that exceptionally fine summer, there were a few anxious days in the valley when the eight fishing boats were out; after a golden morning the wind got up and the outer sea roughened like sackcloth, and the waves came crashing in over the shore stones, peal after peal.

Then there were the anxious women standing here and there on the sea-banks, alone or in small groups, shading their eyes westwards, dumbly willing their men to come back, even if they hadn't a fish to show for the venture and hazard.

Dancey was never among those watchers. 'Fools!' she said. 'The fires'll be out when their men come in cold. What can they do about it? The sea will work as it wants to.'

And the boats came in from the claws of the storm, one after the other. As they passed the croft of Strom, going on home, the women would look askance at the door. What kind of a woman was she, who seemingly had no care or keeping of her man, and was so completely acquiescent in the will of the sea, whether it was benign or murderous?...

Then when Andrew came up, tired and soaked with salt, she would make room for him beside the hearth, and break the peat into yellow flames, and say, 'How many fish did you catch? Half a basket—it could be worse. You fool, could you not have seen the storm coming?'... Then she would heat ale in a pot, and add sugar. While he drank, the bitter incense of sea rose up slowly from his trousers and jersey and boots.

And Dancey, up to her elbows in oatmeal, bent and kissed little Willa who had nipped a finger in the jamb of the door.

In one or two of the crofts, a woman would be saying to her fisherman that she was similarly warming with hot ale and peat flames, 'What do you expect? She isn't one of us. A foreigner from God knows where. None of us will ever be able to understand her. Hard on her man and on her bairns. But she does keep them well fed and well clad, that's true...'

A generation, a slow ponderous wave of time, had gone over the island and the valley since the winter of the shipwreck, and it had taken away many of the older folk, including the old people of Eard, into whose end-of-Yule celebration the child of the sea had been carried with a small flicker of life in it.

Up at Eard lived William Ness, a bachelor, who farmed his few acres and had little to do with the other folk of the valley. He lived by himself, a careful secretive man. Not even a tinker was suffered over his threshold; only the missionary, and the laird's factor when he came for the twice-yearly rent. Children were sent away gruffly. Young women, going up that way with buckets to the spring, had to go through the deep heather behind the house.

William Ness looked after his few beasts and acres tolerably well. But he never went out fishing. After his father died, the boat *Swift* lay on the noust and began slowly to warp. Now she was a poor shrivelled husk beside the eight well-kept fish-seekers of the shore.

On a Sunday he would put on his dark suit and take his Bible and go to the kirk five miles away. But always alone, never one of the little groups of worshippers here and there on the road. Remote and stern, he listened to the sermon. During the prayers, he drooped his head a little. He did not open his mouth during the hymns and psalms. He would place one penny gravely in the collection plate, going in.

A strange lonely man. Yet the valley

people accepted him, as the valley had accepted all kinds of people for hundreds of years since the first ox had dragged a plough through the heather. Nature in individual men and women was as unpredictable as the sea.

And the wave of time had carried away Madge Selquoy, the foster-mother to the shipwrecked child, but not before the child had been reared and nurtured and instructed in all the ways needful for an island girl to know.

There had been a few initial difficulties. What name was Madge to call the child? The child was about a year old; she must have a name, but there was no means of knowing what name she had been given. The ship was so broken up that only her port of registration, Danzig, was found carved on a timber. Danzig the child was called too, when the minister came to christen her. And there was another complication, for nobody could tell whether the bairn from the sea was Catholic, Lutheran, Orthodox or Jewish. Drops of water were sprinkled on its head, and Mary Danzig cried a little, then slept.

'And mercy me,' said old Philip of Graybigging, 'once the bairn comes to the age of speaking, what way will we know what she's saying, and her with a foreign tongue in her head?'

But when Dancey was two years old or thereby—her birthday would forever be a mystery too—she spoke the slow lilting cadances of the other valley children, a language touched with a slight melancholy: Scots-English words thrown upon a loom of ancient Norn.

And Dancey mingled freely with the children of the valley, and all went well in their work and play. But always this aura of mystery clung to her.

An upsurge of time brought together the girl Dancey and Andrew Crag, the crofter-fisherman, whose father had fallen from the crag to his death going after gull eggs five years since, and whose mother was 'wearing away' in the deep chair beside the hearth fire. The old woman put bitter looks on Dancey when Andrew first brought her to Strom, in the way of courtship. She had been kind to Dancey when Dancey was a child and a young girl. But to have another woman sharing her little kingdom! It was a hurtful thing. 'That foreign slut!' she would mumble, but loud enough for the girl to hear. Once the old woman opened her eyes and there was Andrew kissing the girl goodnight in the open door, with a star out beyond them, cold and brilliant. 'Andrew Crag!' she said harshly, 'this was a decent house always. It is my house—Strom belongs to me. You leave here this very night. Go. Go and live with that creature, whoever she is...'

But in the morning she had no memory of what she had seen or said. She knew that her thread was fraying. She would not take to her bed—bed was the next stage to coffin and grave. She ruled the little house of Strom, grim and feeble, from her chair beside the fire.

'I can't go to the fishing and leave her,' said Andrew. 'What am I to do?'

Dancey rolled up her sleeves and came down and milked the cow of Strom and fed the few hens. Whenever she entered the house the old one muttered darkly. She would shake her fist, but feebly, for the strength was out of it.

'You'd feel better after a wash,' said Dancey.

'I'm cleaner than ever you were in your life,' said the old woman.

'I'll make a little porridge,' said Dancey. 'Then you'll feel stronger.'

'Don't touch anything in this house!' came the thin cracked voice. 'I'm not hungry. Don't put a finger on pot or plate.'

She drowsed. And when she woke, she did consent to sip a cup of warm milk. 'Thank you, Andrina,' she said. 'That's

228

kind.' (Andrina was the name of her younger sister who had died of measles twenty years before.) Then she nodded off to sleep.

'I'll help you into bed,' said Dancey.

I'm not ready for bed yet,' said Mrs Crag. 'I feel more comfortable in this chair.'

She drowsed, and woke in an hour. 'Where's Andrew?' she muttered. 'Where's that boy? Is he home from the school yet?'

'Andrew's out in the boat,' said Dancey. 'He'll be home at sunset.'

'He's taken money out of the chest where I was keeping it. The chest under the bed. A shilling now and half-a-sovereign again. The money I was keeping for my wedding...' And she wept: soft easy soundless tears, to think that her son should take her dowry, last precious thing, from her.

'Who are you?' she said to Dancey another day. 'It's kind of you to come. Yes, that's more comfortable, the way you've put the cushions. There was a woman here today—did you see her?—a tinker wife. She stole the china teapot from the sideboard, the one I got for my wedding from the missionary's wife.'

'The teapot's still there, mother,' said Dancey. 'Look!'

'Well, there was a woman here and she was trying to take something. She thought I was asleep. But I was watching her all the time.'

Dancey took the wet warm flannel to her face while she slept and dried her gently.

Mrs Crag woke when Andrew came in with a full basket of haddocks, lurching with it in a kind of slow heavy dance from door to corner. The thump of the basket on the stone floor wakened her.

'Oh Simon!' she cried. 'You never had a catch like that! Your tea's on the table. Come over to the fire and warm you first. Simon, I've built up a fine fire for you. Look!'

The golden hearth shadows were all over the interior of Strom. (Simon had been her husband's name.)

'Simon,' she said, 'I never knew we had a lass—a daughter. She's been with me all day.'

'You should be in your bed, getting a good rest,' said Andrew. 'You've never left that chair for ten days past.'

The old woman considered this for a while.

'So that's it,' she said darkly. 'Once I'm in bed I'm finished. I'm out in the ebb. You can send for Tom Stanger anytime, once you get me in bed. First bed, then coffin. Then everything's yours, the house and land and boat and the money under the bed. You're cruel. While I'm in this chair, there's nothing you can do, you jailbird!'

Exhausted by her spate of words, her head drooped again.

While she slept, Dancey heated broth for Andrew and he ate it with buttered oatcakes, and afterwards beef and tatties.

He kept glancing miserably over at the chair where his mother was ripening for death, so slowly and mysteriously.

That night Dancey did carry her over to her wooden box-bed. But when she woke at dawn she flared up, like a lamp in a draught. 'I'm not dead!' she shrilled. 'I'll live longer than any of you...'

And when Dancey carried her over to her chair beside the reinvigorated hearth, she said, 'I have a lot of things to do in this place before I go.'

Andrew cried a little. Dancey had never seen the glister on his cheeks before. He turned away from her, put on his seaboots and oilskin. Then he kissed his mother and went out quickly.

'Who was that man?' said the old one.

She even, that morning, took two or three spoons of thin porridge from Dancey's hand. 'That was right good,' she said. 'Did you make it? Well, I pay you well enough for anything you do. Why are

231

you neglecting the fire? It's very cold.'

Dancey piled peat on the hearth until it could hold no more. Still the old one complained of the cold.

Outside, the first daffodils were beginning to open in the schoolhouse garden. A few new lambs cried thinly from this field and that.

'I was never so cold,' said old Mrs Crag.

Dancey put the thickest shawl about her shoulders, and broke another peat into the blaze. 'Now then,' she said, 'be good till I come back. I won't be long.'

She went out and across the fields quickly to see if her own ewes had given birth. Her hens came against her in a fierce hungry red wave. Two lambs stottered round their dam in the spring sun. The cow Sybil blew her bugle again and again, 'Milking time!'

Dancey took some honey in a cup back to Strom: honey, if she could sip it, might put some strength into Mrs Crag.

No, she didn't want honey, or anything. 'My mouth's frozen, I can't open it. I only remember one coldness like this, and that's the night they took the bodies out of the ship in the snow. I never saw coldness like that. There's a white shawl in the kist, put it on me. The dead woman in the barn of Eard! And then they brought the bairn in,

232

out of the drifts. I was young then, not long married. I remember thinking, "Poor thing, you'd be better dead." There was life in it still. Whether it lived or died I don't know. I can't remember...'

She took a spoonful of brandy, though half of it ran down her whiskered chin.

'Where's that boy?' she whispered. 'What I'd like Andrew to do is, I'd like him to buy a shop in Hamnavoe with the money. He'd be happy then, and his bairns after him. This crofting and fishing's a poor life. In Hamnavoe, Andrew'll get a good respectable wife. Her hands would be clean always.'

When the sounds of the first ebb were all along the shore, the old woman said, 'I'm tired. I want to go to bed now.'

Before Dancey could get to her, she slumped sideways in her chair. She was dead when Dancey laid her out on the bed.

That evening Tom Stanger came with his tape measure and boards.

Word was sent to the gravedigger, the doctor, the registrar and the missionary.

In every croft curtains were drawn. In the rich spring light, the valley would be blind till after the funeral.

Before midsummer Andrew Crag and Mary Danzig Selquoy were married in the barn of Strom.

The wave of time went over the valley, and removed Shalder the beachcomber and the laird's shepherd and Tom Stanger the joiner-boatbuilder-undertaker. Somebody else had to make Tom's coffin.

And William Ness sat up at Eard, and worked his fields, unbeholden to anyone.

Sometimes the harvests were good enough, and sometimes they were poor, but mostly they were adequate, no more. The people drew most of their food from the sea.

And time broke upon the valley, a slow wave, and carried away the old and the fated, but brought new children, scattering them in this croft and that. In the croft of Strom, the cradle in the corner was rarely empty. After twelve years, from the furthest side of the valley could be heard the medley all weekend from inside Strom, laughter and lamentation and chastisement and encouragement.

Andrew Crag came home from the sea day after day and a wave of children broke about his knee.

'A poor catch that, on a fine fishing day! What ailed you, man?...' And the small boy Stephen, who was clinging too hard to his father's knee, was sent reeling away by a mild sweep from Dancey's open palm. The

234

child in the cradle then would join its thin wail to the yells of Stephen. And the other children would laugh all about the shrill anguish.

'A fisherman needs patience,' said Andrew mildly. 'I'll tell you something else—that boat of mine won't last much longer. She's dangerous in a heavy sea. Tom would have patched her to serve for a year or two yet. What way can I buy a new boat?...'

Dancey set a bowl of broth before him on the bare scrubbed table.

'It'll be a fair to middling harvest,' she said. 'Nothing to speak about. It's a good thing I'm here, to see to it. Or we'd starve here at Strom.'

There came the summer of the golden harvest that was spoken about for a generation afterwards.

That year the elements of sun and rain and wind were so exquisitely measured and scattered upon the furrows that the little black-ploughed fields sown with barley and oats had shallow pools of green soon and then the sloping rectangles were all green, all crammed with murmurings and whisperings in the wayward wind of early summer, and jewelled after a shower; and at morning and evening the lark stood high above the ripening stalks, and the blue hemisphere rang with the rapture of its singing.

The valley folk waited anxiously; many a year such promise had been ruined by a week-long deluge of August rain. And if an easterly wind came with the rain, a whole summer of work could be all but ruined.

The weather kept faith with the crofters. The corn changed overnight, from green to bronze, not uniformly, but croft by croft would receive the blessing. Then, after the pledge and seal of the sun, it was time to put the scythes in.

It did not take the cockerel to wake them, those late summer mornings.

The crofters did not wait for their own ripening time. Whenever a field took the burnish, there they all went with their scythes, and before dark the last stook was set up.

There were a few grumbles here and again. 'That's not fair! It should be our field for cutting in the morning, not theirs!' (Mostly it was the women who complained.)

The men would sit down under a stook, smoking their pipes, and discuss the rotation mildly. The women would pour ale out of the great stone jar—and usually before they dispersed it had been agreed whose field was next for cutting.

Always they cocked their heads, hearkening for a smell or taste of rain on the wind. A few of the older men and women knew days before whether it would rain, and they always took into their calculation the airt of the wind and the phase of the moon. Even the sun held portents; too clear and intense a light portended prolonged rain, and that very soon. The best promise was a faint bloom of haar, or mist, along the horizon at morning and evening.

Day after day of faintly diffused sunlight fell into the valley, and flashed from the swinging scythes of the harvesters. The swathes fell before them. The women followed after, gathering and binding. The children ran among the stooks, chasing rabbits and birds. There was no school till harvest was over.

There among the harvesters laboured the squat strong figure of Dancey. Only she did not stoop and gather like the other women; she swung a scythe with the men. With keen crisp susurrations the line of scythes went through the dense coroneted barley.

Old Billo Spence the ex-sailor licked his finger and held it up to the wind. His nostril flared. 'No rain for the next few days,' said he... The harvesters let Billo go home early, for he was crippled with

237

rheumatics and couldn't keep up with the other men.

A child from the croft of Svert wailed suddenly! A bee had stung him.

All the crofters worked together, in this field and that, except William Ness of Eard. William Ness had never been beholden to anybody. William Ness cut his own harvest. Let them keep to their own fields. Let the women especially keep away from his acres, with their gossip and inquisitiveness.

Sometimes the harvesters would cast an eye up at Eard. The oatfield there was ripe for cutting all right—in fact one corner had been cut—but there was no sign of the solitary harvester. He must be all right, as far as anything could be right with the creature, for his door was standing open. But his cow in the field above was raising a great outcry.

The day dawned clear and fresh for cutting the two fields of Strom. The harvesters arrived, singly and in groups. Dancey had porridge and boiled eggs and bannocks on the table for them, 'to give them strength'... Andrew she sent to the fishing—'he would be nothing but a hindrance'. She swung her scythe for an hour or two, but she had to break off every now and again to go inside and get more food ready for the harvesters,

238

and replenish the ale jar, and see to the infant in the cradle. The valley children had never had a day like it, leaping back from the flash and onset of the scythes, hurling themselves on the threefold stooks, chasing the rabbits that leaped and danced from their diminishing domain.

Once or twice Dancey, coming out with the cheese and oatcakes and ale jar, cast her eye up at the croft of Eard and its bellowing cow.

'There's something wrong there,' she said.

The harvesters shrugged their shoulders. He had never needed them. Let him see still to his own affairs.

Andrew Crag came up from the shore with a full basket of crabs. The children were too steeped in bronze and ripeness that afternoon to pay much attention to him. 'I think it'll come to rain,' said Andrew. 'But not for a day or two.' He held out a mug to be filled with ale. 'Get inside,' cried Dancey.

By sunset the two fields were cut. The harvesters trooped home on half a dozen different paths.

Dancey put on her coat and took the steepest path up the hill.

'Get out,' yelled William Ness from the floor. 'Nobody asked you to come here.'

239

He was lying on a rag mat near the dead hearth, with his right leg splayed at a wrong angle.

'Get out,' he shouted. 'I fell, that's all. I tripped on a stone out there in the field and came down. I'll get up again when I'm ready.'

'Your leg's broken,' said Dancey. 'You need the doctor.'

'I want no doctor,' said William Ness. 'The leg'll mend. I can't afford doctors.'

'I don't care about you,' said Dancey. 'You can die for all I care. That poor cow of yours, Queenie, she needs milking. Listen to her. She's in agony.'

'Milk her,' said William. 'Then go.'

'And your hens are starving,' said Dancey. 'Where do you keep your oats?'

When Dancey had milked the cow and fed the hens, she came back and rekindled the dead fire.

'How long have you been lying here?' she asked.

'A day and a night,' said the man. 'I had just begun to cut the oats when I fell over that stone. Leave the fire alone.'

Dancey plied the bellows and the fire was all roaring yellow and red rags.

'I've just told Jacob Voe,' she said. 'Jacob's gone over the hill to get the doctor.'

'This house is private property,' said the

240

man. 'You're trespassing. The laird will hear about this.'

'You must be hungry,' said Dancey. 'Let's see what you have in your cupboard.'

'You slut,' he muttered.

'O Lord, what misery!' cried Dancey from the open cupboard. 'A few bits of salt fish. A few tatties. Some mouldy oatmeal. I knew you were mean, but I little thought it was as miserable as this. I'll go home and get some hot broth for you.'

'You'll go home and you'll never darken this door again!' cried the man on the floor.

'I'll boil an egg or two in the meantime,' said Dancey. 'I'd better be here when the doctor comes.'

She boiled three eggs and shelled them and emptied them into a bowl, after blowing the peat dust out of it. Then she set the bowl of salted eggs down beside William Ness, with a horn spoon in it. 'Eat,' she said.

He wouldn't touch the spoon. He wouldn't even look at it.

'House-breaking,' he said. 'This is a serious business. A matter for the police.'

'I'm not going to force it down your throat,' said Dancey. 'If you want to die of starvation, you can. You've had plenty of practice.'

She found a broom behind the door and

set about sweeping the floor all round the stricken man. 'We can't let the doctor see a hovel like this. I expect he's seen many a poor place in his time, but never a pigsty like this...' Sometimes she swept a spider's web with the broom from the rafters, or a hanging curtain of smoky filth from above the hearth.

'The doctor might be able to save your leg—it's hard to say,' said Dancey. 'The eggs are cold. But eat them. You'll need all your strength.'

The man closed his eyes, as if he were sleeping. But from time to time he moaned a little.

'Sore, is it?' said Dancey. 'Just wait till Dr McCrae begins to put you together again.'

It was time to light the lamp. Dancey 'tut-tutted' while she scoured the greasy lampglass with her apron, and trimmed the wick, and shook the bowl to see how much oil there was in it. 'I don't suppose it's been lit since last winter,' she said. 'And then only for a few minutes till you read your chapter and got into bed.'

They heard the clip-clop of hooves, the rattle of wheels, from the throat of the valley a mile away.

When Dr McCrae arrived the inside of Eard was softly irradiated.

They heaved William Ness, moaning, on

to his bed. 'A good thing you found him when you did,' said Dr McCrae. 'Another night and he'd have been a gonner. Now, man, this is going to hurt you. Dancey, would you put on some water to boil? Your oat-field?—it's your leg I'm worried about, man, not your oat-field. You'll be lucky if you can hobble as far as the door this side of Hallowe'en. Dancey, if you open my bag you'll find a big blue bottle with tablets in it. Yes, take it over...'

Next morning, Dancey left the neighbour woman Angela in charge of the children of Strom. She took a can of hot broth across the burn and up the side of the hill to Eard. She pushed open the door.

'Here's some soup, man,' said Dancey. 'If I can find a bowl that's passing clean. Broth like this'll have you on your feet in no time. Tell me if you want more salt in it. Here.'

William Ness let on not to be aware of her existence. He lay in the box-bed with his eyes lightly closed. He could have been dead but for the faint flutter at his lips and the pulse in his temple.

'I'll set it on the chair then,' said Dancey. 'When you're hungry, you'll eat. I'm not going to coax you.'

The man on the bed said nothing.

'Every cornfield's cut except yours,' said

243

Dancey. 'It's a poor thin crop, like the man that sowed it. But it's a pity to let it lie waste. The rain's coming, Andrew says.'

She took the scythe out of the barn and whetted it on a stone and set about cutting the oat-field of Eard. By mid-afternoon it was all finished—the field cut and the stocks set up. She had done it alone. It was a very small field.

When Dancey went into the house to tell William Ness that his harvest was cut, he was still lying there with his eyes closed. The bowl of broth lay cold on the chair next to the bed, with the horn spoon lying in it.

'I suppose better men have died of starvation,' said Dancey. 'Anyway, your field's cut.'

Before she went home, she took in a bucket of water from the spring. 'Tomorrow, I'll tidy you up,' she said. 'The doctor and the missionary'll be coming to see you. I'll leave the broth. Even if it's cold it's nourishing enough.'

As Dancey went in at the door of Strom, she heard the clip-clop of the doctor's gig coming on the road between the hills.

Down at the shore, Andrew was setting his basket of fish on a flat rock. The sun took silver flashings from them.

William Ness lay as quiet as a corpse, but

for the flutter of a nostril, while Dancey poured water from bucket into basin, and unwrapped a piece of green soap from a flannel. 'I ought to heat the water,' she said. 'But the cold water might put a spark of life in you.'

When she wet the flannel and soaped it to wash his face, he swung at her with his fist. The blow caught Dancey off balance and she reeled against the bedpost. 'Ah!' said Dancey, 'that's what I like to see. You're mending. You're getting your strength back.'

She wound one fist through his grey-black hair and held his head down on the pillow, and with the other hand she washed his face thoroughly. Once he tried to bite her—she took the cold flannel and whipped it across his mouth. 'You've got ten good years of life in you yet,' said Dancey, 'with all that strength.' Her flannelled finger went into his ear-whorls and nose-flanges. Then she took the towel to him and rubbed so hard that he let out a soft moan. 'I've brought a comb too,' said Dancey.

He made no resistance while she combed his beard and his hair. 'You'd be a bonny enough man,' she said, 'if only you kept yourself clean and tidy. What you need is a wife. I don't suppose any lass in this island would have you. But if you were to put an advertisement in the *Orkney Herald*...'

When she saw tears oozing out of his closed eyes, and glittering in his eye-pouches, Dancey said she'd go out and milk his cow. 'I think what you need is a mug of warm milk and a couple of eggs.'

He would not eat or drink, still. She left the milk and the new-boiled eggs and the oatcakes on the chair beside the bed, growing cold. 'The bairns'll be home for their dinner. I'll be back in the afternoon.'

He had bitten his lower lip so fiercely that a bead of blood stood there.

When Dancey returned in the late afternoon, William Ness was asleep. He hadn't touched the milk or the food. The pure breath of sleep came from his mouth, soft and rhythmic—he looked like a boy lost in the wonderment of falling snow. Dancey kissed him on the forehead. Then softly she left the house. She milked Queenie the cow in the upper field; then she went home.

When she returned in the morning, he was awake. The mug and the plate were empty.

'Well done!' cried Dancey. 'You'll get a fresh haddock for your tea. I should change your bed today. Are there blankets in that kist?'

'I don't want your charity,' said William.

'I'll pay you for the work you've done. There's a black box at the foot of the cupboard, far back. Be good enough to bring it here to me. The key is behind that loose stone in the wall—yes, that one. Bring it, too.'

He unlocked the little black lacquered box and inside, in separate compartments, were gold coins and banknotes. The sovereigns spilled from his fingers back into the box, golden music. The notes looked like discarded mummy wrappings and had an ancient smell.

'How much do I owe you for your services, up to now?' said William Ness.

Dancey laughed. 'Lock it all away,' she said. 'You'll need it all to pay the undertaker and the gravedigger, and for the funeral whisky.'

Treasure-box and key were restored to their separate secret places.

'You're a very strange woman,' said William Ness.

The cow Queenie lowed from the field above.

When Dancey returned with the pail of milk, he said, 'My leg is not so painful today.'

He drank the warm milk so eagerly that his whiskers were festooned with white droplets.

As Dancey was leaving, he said in a

low voice, 'I think I would like a piece of haddock with butter about it, and a bannock.'

Dancey met the missionary on the sheep path. 'He's getting stronger every day,' she said. 'He'll be very pleased to see you for a change.'

Before the month was out, William Ness was on his feet again; though he hirpled on a stick for the rest of the winter.

One morning Dancey said, 'You can do for yourself now, can't you? You can milk Queenie and light your fire? And take in peats and water from the spring? Then I'll be off.'

'Thank you, woman,' he said.

Dancey never crossed the threshold of Eard again.

It was plain to be seen by all in the course of the next winter that the croft reverted slowly to its former state of filth and neglect. The little windows lost the glitterings Dancey had put on them. But on a Sunday morning William Ness emerged from that withered door in his black suit with his Bible under his arm, and set out slowly on his staff to the kirk five miles away.

The accident had not put one drop of honey into his nature. He did his slow business—if he had to—with the other valley folk curtly and ungraciously. If a child wandered near his door, he would swipe at it with his stick and utter some wild meaningless syllable. On winter nights the valley boys threw stones against his door. One night of snow a stone went through his window. Two days later the policeman from Hamnavoe arrived in the valley and sharply interrogated the pupils in the school. A policeman come for them! They were grey as cinders in the face at the thought of chains and dungeons.

The boy who had broken the window was never discovered.

And Dancey: for William Ness it was, between him and her, what it had always been, as if the affair of the broken leg had never happened. If they chanced to meet, on the peat road or along the shore, he would look through her as if she was made of glass.

Dancey always had a few words for him. 'It's time you were getting a new cow, man. Queenie is done...' 'Have you put that advertisement in the paper yet for a bride?...' 'Watch yourself in this snow—it's very slippery up at the spring...'

Never an answer. He had ears of stone, going past her with the limp he always had now since he broke his leg.

As Dancey had predicted, William Ness

lived for ten more years. Then, when no smoke was seen from his chimney for three mornings in April, the shepherd from the big house found him slumped in his chair, with a cold smile on his face, and a spider spinning a web between his dropped hand and the wall.

Only as many men as were required to carry the coffin attended the funeral. Andrew Crag was at the fishing that afternoon.

A month later the postman from the island post office five miles away walked down the valley with a letter for Andrew Crag, esquire, Strom. The address was typewritten, the flap of the envelope had a red embossed seal to it.

Andrew opened the letter with trembling fingers (a letter like this boded no good).

It was from the solicitor in Kirkwall. 'Dear Sir, I enclose a copy of the will of the late William Ness, of Eard. I should be glad if you could come to our office in Kirkwall as soon as possible, to sign the necessary forms and finalise the business. Yours faithfully...'

William Ness's will was short and simple. 'I leave all my worldly goods and assets to Andrew Crag of Strom in this island, to get him a new boat. Any man with a wife like he has got, with her clattering tongue and her interferences, deserves to be out of the house as often as he can, among the silences of the sea. His old boat *Hopeful* is the worse for wear. Let Andrew Crag order a new boat from the yard in Hamnavoe. Whatever monies are left over to be equally divided among his children, the poor man...'

Shell Story

The seagulls came to the island pier.

The old wives came out with bowls, with crusts and bits of fat in them.

They threw the scraps to the gulls.

While the food still hung in the blue air, the gulls gobbled every fragment up.

'That's Tommy Ritch, that gull, that's my Tommy,' said one old woman, pointing to a gull that was stretching his wings on the pier. 'Tommy got his death off Yesnaby thirty-one years ago come June.'

'Here you come again, Willie Anderson,' said another old wife. 'Look at him gobbling up that hen giblet. He was always hungry when he came in from the sea. My neighbour Willie, he was lost on the trawler *Nevis,* a long while ago.'

'I think that gull is my brother Drew,' said one old woman. 'But I was only two when his ship went down off Iceland. So I don't remember him. I can't tell if it is Drew or not.'

So the old wives spoke to the gulls after every dinnertime, calling them by the names of drowned fishermen and sailors that were kin or acquaintances.

One old wife, Charlotte, looked every afternoon into the gull-shrieking, gull-beating air over the village and every afternoon she shook her head. She could never see her man Jock Wylie in the white screaming gull-drift. Jock Wylie had gone down in unknown seas, the winter after they were married... Still Charlotte threw bits of bannock and bits of bacon to the gulls... And Charlotte was getting on for a hundred years old.

Still the village wives kept up their singsong.

'Here's a piece of bread for you, Bertie Ness...'

'You like chicken wings, don't you, Ally Flett? Take it...'

'I swear, Jerry Thomson, you're a greedier gull than you were a ferryman...'

'I bet you'd sooner have beer than this end of bacon, Dickie Folster...'

Old Charlotte threw her scraps to the gulls and viewed every one from her shaded eyes, and shook her head and went home.

One day there was such a storm that even the gulls kept to their crag ledges in the Black Craig.

Oh, it was a howling gale out of the east!

The fishermen and their wives and

253

children stayed inside, behind their rattling doors.

They saw through their salt-crusted windows a woman struggling down to the pier. They thought every moment she would be blown into the white-crested waves. And, 'It's Charlotte!' they cried in croft after croft.

Then the village folk saw that a solitary bird had fallen and furled on the very edge of the stone pier.

Old Charlotte took a piece of fine cake that she had kept from the last island wedding, full of fruit and nuts, fine flour and rum, and she put it into the seabird's beak. It seemed to be a bigger bird than the usual gull.

The bird ate the bridecake, and it flew three times round Charlotte's head, and then it swung away out to the open sea.

And the wind blew salt spray over the roofs.

The old woman knocked at every door along the village street.

When the man of the house tugged the door open—so fierce the gale blew—Charlotte said in a young sweet voice, 'Jock my man, he's come back to see me at last from the wastes of ocean.'

The Architect

JANUARY

It was the highest honour for me, Fergus, master mason in Aberdeen, to get a message from the famous Sweyn Asleifson that he needed my services urgently.

A dangerous passage, in the depths of winter, on an Iceland merchant vessel, to Orkney.

There I stood at last, in an easterly gale, on the shore of Gairsay, Sweyn Asleifson's island.

The great pirate, friend of kings and earls, was older by a hundred grey beard-bristles than when I had last seen him in the courtyard of a keep in Kinnaird, one winter ten years before.

He uses few courtesies, Sweyn.

'I hear you're a good man with stone,' he said. 'I want a new stone house here, with barn and byres, soon. A man can't live for ever.'

The Orkney chiefs, their long halls and outhouses have always been timber built: a habit their ancestors brought from Norway

255

and were reluctant to abandon, though for centuries (Orkney being treeless) the wood had to be imported from Norway or Scotland.

There is an abundance of good building stone in the islands.

There is a dangerous tradition among the Orkneymen too. Whenever a dispute breaks out between families, one or other of the rival houses may go up in flames. Earls and sea-lords have ended among red embers and smoke, with their doors barred from outside so that only the servants could get out; and a few charred skulls were strewn about the hot stones next morning.

Sweyn of Gairsay, though he was a friend of earls and kings, from Norway to Ireland, had many enemies.

Now, in old age, he was mindful of dying peaceably in bed, in a house of good stone.

I rejoiced that there might soon be plenty of work for quarrymen and stoneworkers all over the north, from Caithness to Shetland, once Sweyn's example was followed, as it certainly would be.

'That can be done, my lord,' I said. (I have learned to know my place, and to be adept at flattery, therefore I called this formidable man 'my lord'.) 'It will take a year or two to build a long hall worthy of such a man as Sweyn Asleifson. A quarry will have to be opened, and blocks levered out and dressed. A solid foundation must be laid. So I'll have to send to Scotland for a few good masons and a reliable gang of labourers. The work, if all goes well, should be finished the summer after next.'

'I want the new building finished by next Yule,' said Sweyn Asleifson. 'And I don't want my island invaded by a rabble out of Scotland. I keep eighty men here in Gairsay—ploughmen, shepherds, fishermen, fowlers, seamen. They're idle a lot of the time. They will do the labouring work. They opened a new quarry near the cliff last winter. You can start at once.'

'But, my lord...' said I (and my heart itself was like a stone that day).

'Don't "my lord" me,' said the old man. 'I'm just old Sweyn, a plain farmer and sailor. If you can't build this hall and steading for me, I'll have to send to Lübeck or Bergen for a builder with more smeddum. What's your answer? A plain yes or no.'

As it happened, I had no choice in the matter. It blew up into one of those fierce week-long gales, when only fools and pilgrims travel.

I inspected the site. I drew a rough plan on parchment. The ale horn was comforting at midnight, when the storm howled across Gairsay, Rousay, Wyre, Egilsay, night after night.

It is impossible that this work should be done in nine months.

FEBRUARY

Two old men growling at one another over supper.

The bishop arrived from his little cathedral in Birsay this morning.

I was working at the parchment plan of the new hall and steading, at the far end of the board; a candle splash on the charcoal marks.

'You have not introduced me to your guest,' said Bishop William to Sweyn Asleifson.

'I forget his name,' said Sweyn. 'He's neither here nor there. A Scottish mason. He's here to build a new house.'

'My name is Fergus, your grace,' I called from the far end of the table. 'I have built several good houses, as far south as Fife.'

'What does an old man like you want with a new mansion?' said the bishop to Sweyn. 'It's about time you set your mind to your everlasting house, it won't be long till you need it—"a house not made with hands, eternal in the heavens..." '

'I pay you tithes. I light a candle on Magnus Day. I say a prayer when I remember. I look after my people here in Gairsay. I don't want to die among fires and smoke. A good stone house will last for centuries.'

A girl came with a jug and mugs of ale for the two ancients.

'Everyone in Orkney, even the earl, is afraid of you, Sweyn,' said the bishop. 'Only I speak plain to you. Your farmhouse is a safe place, the best in Orkney, it will never be a nest of flames. A new stone mansion is vanity. What you need here in Gairsay is a little church, both for yourself and your islanders. You are an old man near death. You have spent your life in pillage and robbery and wounding in the Atlantic, as far south as Scilly. It's high time you washed all that blood from your hands, before you die. Have Fergus build you a stone church, with a font and a niche for holy water. So, you can sign yourself with a cross of bright water, under an arch, before you die.'

'See to your business and I will do the things I have to do,' said Sweyn, and the wolf growl was in his voice.

Then he suddenly shouted the length of the table to me, 'You get on with your work too, stone howker. I've noticed, the new quarry isn't exactly a beehive of industry.'

I rolled up my parchment, blew out my candle, and went to the room that I share with Sweyn's farm manager and his blacksmith (who makes more axes and daggers than horseshoes.) They are agreeable men. We throw dice in the evenings.

How can stone be quarried in these winter blizzards?

But I have the new hall and barn and stable and byre well sketched. Even on the parchment it is a thing of beauty. Only it can never be built in time for the Harvest Home.

MARCH

Work went well at the new quarry, in the growing sun of March.

The farmworkers, fishermen, shepherds of Gairsay became quarrymen. They learned to dress the stone, and we had hundreds of blocks stacked under the one hill of Gairsay.

Every noon the women brought bread and ale to the site.

This kind of stone is beautiful to look at and easy to cut, but it is friable and will not weather well in this climate. The salt wind will eat into it. It is not like the hard glittering granite of Aberdeen.

One morning the labourers did not turn up at the quarry.

Instead, I heard a great noise of hammering, sawing, scraping in the shed where Sweyn's longship *Wild Goose* had been laid up for the winter.

They told me at the door of the shed, 'It's time for the spring cruise. We're making the ship ready.'

Earlier in the month, I had been a bit short-handed, because Sweyn's great field had had to be ploughed and seeded, and the shepherds had been busy night and day on the hill at lambing-time, and the fishing-boats had been out after ling and cod, to be smoked and salted.

But always a dozen or so had turned up at the quarry, and mallet and chisel were never idle.

Today, there was nobody at the quarry but myself.

Sweyn Asleifson was in high good humour, going between the hall and the boatshed twenty times a day, giving orders and commands. Even his anger had a kind of boisterous gaiety in it.

At last rollers were put down and *Wild Goose* was dragged from her shed into the sea, glistening black with new tar. Mast and steering oar had been painted deep red. She rode at anchor, a beautiful bird.

Then the women carried on board baskets of smoked fowl and fish and hard oatbread and casks of ale.

Fishermen and ploughmen and shepherds and fowlers came out of their huts and hovels rigged for a long sea voyage, in leather breeches and jackets, and bonnets of thick well-oiled wool.

One by one, the 'vikings' (who yesterday had been island yokels) waded out to the ship. Sweyn was pulled on board last. I have never seen an old man so merry. There was a piper on board. Sweyn laughed among the crew, he even put his arm round this one and that. He gave the signal for the sail to be raised. There was a brisk wind from northeast.

The women of Gairsay stood along the shore as quiet as stones.

I stood a little apart from them.

Sweyn noticed me. 'You, quarry man,' he cried, 'see that my new house and steading are in place when we get back from Atlantis.'

The wind filled the sail. *Wild Goose* drifted slowly between Rousay and the Island of Horses, with music and cheering, out into the open Atlantic.

The women waited and watched till she was out of sight, then they trooped back silently to their duties in the great hall.

Only one girl was left, Gretl. She was weeping silently because the blacksmith's boy, Vald, had gone on the ship: his first voyage.

Now I was alone on this island of women, commanded to build a splendid house and steading before winter set in.

I thought often of Isabel, the merchant's beautiful daughter in Aberdeen.

APRIL

Suddenly, in April, the island became beautiful with new grass and troops of marigolds along the burn, and larks mounting so high that they seemed to be lost and dissolved in their own raptures. Lambs fluttered everywhere about the high fields. Simply to walk and breathe the sweet boreal air was a delight.

You will say, 'What joy, to be one young man in an island of women, in the springtime of the year!...'

The women of Gairsay were not in the least interested in me. Since the departure of *Wild Goose,* young and old they went about their duties as if their hearts were consumed with an inner rage, like slow-burning embers of charcoal. It seemed to me that they were jealous of the sea for taking their men from them. They were embittered at their men for going after this temptress who allured them, year after year, with promise of riches and fame, but the truth was that often enough they came home, one lacking a leg, or a great wound was on another that presently coiled roots about his heart, and flowered in terrible festerings and the seaman was dead before Yule. Or a wave plucked this one and that, and dragged them under, and they were never seen again.

This was the story of the island, year after year.

But they would not waste a tear or a sigh on such fools. Only little Gretl put the corner of her apron to her eye, sometimes, missing Vald the apprentice blacksmith.

As for me, they set food and ale before me in silence twice a day. And if I ventured so far into April dalliance as to compliment a young woman on the goodness of her smoked trout, and the mellowness of her ale, I got nothing but contemptuous looks from those ice-blue eyes. They had nothing to say to the stranger. Some of the young women were magnificent creatures, with their coils of bronze hair, and their lithe comings and goings here and there about Gairsay, to see to sheep or cows and geese.

I worked alone at the quarry. A few days after the departure of *Wild Goose*, I was joined by a few old men who were too feeble now for viking cruises, and a few young lads with first hairs hardly on their lips.

The old men spent the April days telling about the great cruises they had been on in their day, and how much silver and silk they had brought home to Gairsay. (Where was it all now?) Their hands on mallet and chisel lay light as withered leaves.

An old woman called Svena called from the shore. 'Don't listen to them, Scotsman. They're all liars. My old Finn spent his viking days spewing over the side, a nuisance to everybody!'

Then the old men laughed, water coming from their crinkly eyes; but old Finn shook with rage.

One day in the middle of April all the folk rowed across to the nearby island of Egilsay, to hear the bishop say Mass. It was the feast day of Saint Magnus the Martyr.

I stayed alone at the slowly deepening quarry.

I am not a religious man.

It was springtime—I thought often of Isabel, with pain and sweetness.

MAY

There came a sudden storm one night in May. The timbers of the great house creaked and groaned.

'The Orkneymen need stone houses,' I said, between two sleeps that wild night. 'More than anything they need solid walls and roofs!'

The first I knew of storm trouble was when the girl Gretl was ladling my breakfast porridge. 'Oh,' cried she, 'a wreck at the crag.'

It turned out to be a wreck not worth plundering—a little ship of Irish monks blown off course.

A couple of strakes had been fractured on a rock. There on the shore stood ten shaven heads in long grey sodden cloaks.

It happens that I can speak some Celtic, having built a few big houses in Skye and Barra. (Also I can speak French and English and Norse. Architects don't stay in one place.)

I said to the old monk, 'You won't get your ship repaired. The carpenter's in the west, robbing merchant ships. He won't be back till August.'

'Oh,' said he, 'we can wait. We're in God's hands. We'll be happy here, in this beautiful island. Nothing happens by chance. We were meant to stay awhile in Gairsay.'

'That may be,' said I. 'Only, you should know, the island is full of sharp-tongued grasping women, and they won't be feeding you at their fires.'

'Isn't the sea full of fish?' said he. 'Isn't the cliff alive with birds? We'll draw our little bruised ship on to the sand, and we'll stay there till she's seaworthy again. The name of our ship is *St Brendan...*'

'Where were you headed for,' I said, 'with your cargo of nothingness?'

'We were hoping to get to the Faroes, or Iceland, or Greenland, wherever the winds and waves took us, for light is needed in the dark places of the north. But, see, God has set us ashore on Gairsay.'

Up at the quarry, upon each of the stone blocks I carved my mason's mark, a simple F, for not every house in Alba or the islands can boast of a house built by the master mason Fergus.

Slowly the quarry deepened. I had to listen day after day to the quarrels, grousings, and boasts of the old men as they went wheezing and hirpling among the hewn stones.

The boys were more at the bird cliff and the rock pools than at the quarry. (I would certainly complain about that

267

to Sweyn Asleifson, later.) Usually it was young Gretl who brought the quarrymen food and drink at noon. The old men teased her. She said nothing, day after day. She gathered up the basket and ale bucket and went back to the hall.

We saw nothing of the little community of monks.

But I heard them seven or eight times a day, at their psalms. The first murmurings would reach my ear soon after midnight, monotonous as the wash of sea among shore-stones. Then again, at dawn, if I happened to waken early after an ale-sodden sleep.

There was more muted chanting when I broke my prayerless bread in the morning, and again as I tried to spur my old men and boys into quarrying; four or five times till after the sun went down late, now in early summer.

'It makes a change from the whitemaas and the oyster catchers,' said old Aud.

Meantime a green flush went over the ploughland. There was a sufficiency, an equipoise, of sun and rain, now in early summer.

'It promises to be a good harvest,' said old Borg. 'But I would rather be reaping gold and broadcloth off English ships in Severn-mouth!'

'He was never further than Stroma for

a sack or two of whelks,' sniggered old Svena behind her hand.

The children of Gairsay ran laughing across the meadows.

Then it came on the ripening wind, the mild murmur from the hidden part of the shore, a measured mingling of dark and light voices.

'What are they good for, these men?' I said. 'They could be here at the quarry, helping us with the stones.'

'That's Vespers,' said old Finn, who had once been an altar boy, long ago, at Eynhallow.

JUNE

I was almost as angry as the island women, all the month of June.

Here I was, a young famous master mason, bidden north to undertake a great work, and there was nothing for me to do but superintend a few old men and boys in a quarry, and the men sunk in foolish stories of the past which became more heroic with every telling. What wonderful vikings they had been, at this siege and that sea battle! What beautiful women had been theirs, in Paris and Dublin! Their pouches had been weighty with gold pieces.

The thought of my Isabel, at that time

269

of the year, was a vivid pain to me.

So it went on, day after day, as they dragged an occasional block out of the quarry, and applied the mallets and chisels. If the block was well made, I sealed it with my mason's mark.

June is the month of light in the north, so that it becomes like an over-brimming well. Midnight is only a mild twilight. Sunset in the northwest bequeaths its torch to dayspring in the northeast.

I happened to meet the oldest monk one day at the shore. He said, in his Irish Gaelic, that summer and winter are but a prefiguration of the soul's light and darkness. At winter solstice, the sun seems to be on its death bed. In spring the stone of death is rolled away, and the resurrected sun walks across the earth, bringing plants and animals and fishes and birds and folk in its wake. And now, in high summer, there is no doubt of the supreme victory of the light: all creation flourishes in its abundance. So, in the spiritual domain, was it with Christ and his kingdom.

I said to the old bald-head that there needed no supernatural dimension. The sea ebbs and flows, the moon darkens and rounds out to a fulness, there is snow and the rose... These rhythms in nature are sufficient in themselves. As for a master mason like me: a house crumbles, a new pristine rooftree rises in its place, with a cluster of fine chambers and outhouses, at the architect's bidding.

'Shadows, shadows,' said the old man, smiling, and we parted on the shore.

Meantime the first barley shoots were thrusting through the ploughlands, and the morning meadows lay heavy and cold with dew-laden grass.

I told my old labourers to leave the quarry and the stone-cutting for a day or two. I rounded up the truant boys from the shore... One day of battering rams and we brought the wooden barn down with a great splintering and crashing.

'Plenty of good firewood next winter,' said old Aud.

The boy Hallstein, a grandson of Sweyn Asleifson, returned from the caves to say that the monks were building a kind of a sheepfold or planticru out of shore stones, on the sea-bank above their beached ship.

Then (said the boy) as if a bell unheard had been struck, the dozen brothers dropped whatever they had been doing, and they stood between the broken ship and the half-finished ruckle, and began to sing their Nones.

'And', said the boy, 'they are living on seaweed and whelks and mussels, and they have tamed an otter to bring them fish.'

At this, the old men laughed the child,

Hallstein, to scorn.

So, the bright month of June passed, mostly in idleness.

The great house was like a beehive with the women of Gairsay coming and going, milking and spinning and cheese-making, cooking and scolding and mocking.

Every evening, Gretl climbed to the top of one steep hill and shaded her eyes westward.

We brought the stones down from the quarry to the site where the demolished barn had been. The foundation would do for the new stone barn.

JULY

There is no problem building a barn. Barns have been built since men ceased to be hunters. A loft is necessary for the sacks of corn, a threshing floor, a round kiln for the kernels to be fired for maltings.

They laboured—I directing—at this barn all the month of July. The old men grumbled, shifting and setting the heavy blocks ('We had light Norwegian timber in our time'), the young boys mixed the mortar between laughter and mischief (when they worked at all.) Even I broke into a sweat sometimes, levering a block that was too heavy for the ancients... Some of the strong young women came out and thrust the feebler workers aside, and put in an hour or two on the site, shifting and setting. They listened resentfully when I gave orders, but worked hard to carry them out.

The older women fed us well with fish and bread and ale.

'This is only the start,' I said to the old grumblers at work-break, their beards fleeced with ale foam. 'The big hall has to be built before Sweyn gets back. You'll truly have to put your backs to the work in the next few weeks.'

They glowered at me as the Israelites in Egypt must have turned their dusty faces to Pharaoh's overseer.

We were used now to the monodics from the monks' cave, round at the hidden shore of the island. This eight-fold office throughout the day, made in fact a kind of work pattern for us. I laid down my plumbline or raised my set square in balance with the psalm singing: Prime and Terce and Nones.

Occasionally we heard them shifting shore stones.

In the middle of July—it sometimes happens in the north—there was a rain spate that lasted for three days and nights. The old men refused to work. They kept indoors like wet bees. The women shrieked against them: 'Idle useless creatures!' The women denied them ale—their own grandfathers! The rain came in continuous deluges and torrents.

The children ran about on the hillside with streaming faces and fingers. Sun and rain were equal delights to them.

The green corn drank the cloud-bounty and grew by an inch or two. The island throbbed from end to end with surges and onsets of rain, so heavy and insistent on the third day that I could not hear the murmured formal keenings and rejoicings from the monk-acre.

They are formidable, the island women. Thora, the head woman, gave me a look that would have soured a honeycomb. 'Get the old death-dodgers back to the barn building,' she said. 'The rain will wash a year's grime from them. Why should old men worry about coughs and rheumatics? Do they want to live for ever?'

The old men drank water from the butt, and threw dice. The lintel over the main door ran and teemed with rain beads. Women went in and out to the milking shed. Dry and fire flushed they went out. They came back cold and bright-streaming.

Then, between two rumbles of thunder, I heard it, the sound of shifting stone from the cave.

If nobody else in Gairsay was working, the monks were.

I walked round, after the thunder cloud had rolled on over Kirkvoe, to see what kind of hovel those Irishmen were putting up.

It was still raining hard. A small square building they were putting up, out of blue shore stones, a place little bigger than a fishing bothy. It had two crude transepts. It was to be a chapel for them to sing their psalms in! The first winter storm would blow the place about their ears.

But, considering that they had no proper tools to work with, other than their hands, it was astonishing that the place had got as high even as this. They had actually made a round arch, and two other arches were beginning to incline towards each other, like the two women waiting to embrace in The Visitation.

'No, Fergus,' said the oldest monk, with rain streaming down his face, 'we have never put stone upon stone before. But some of our brothers in Ulster are church builders. And we have watched them. And now we build as the swallow builds her nest, or the bees their hive.'

There was a blue patch in the sky, over Egilsay.

A rainbow arched between Rousay and Eynhallow.

The arch of the little chapel was hung with lingering raindrops. Each raindrop glittered like a jewel.

AUGUST

Early in August, Sweyn Asleifson and his vikings came back to Gairsay.

Sweyn leapt out of the ship into the sea and waded ashore. 'A great voyage!' he shouted. But his face was worn with sun and salt.

The women stood in a broken line above the shore stones.

They know, before the cargo has been uncovered, when a viking cruise has been a failure.

The men waded ashore, starved and exhausted. The young shepherd had to be carried, he had lost a leg below the knee.

'Where's my Rolf?' said Ingi the dark woman. She is the one in charge of the looms and the cloth-making.

'Rolf died a hero's death in Lewis,' said the sailor-blacksmith.

'I didn't like Rolf all that much in the end,' said the weaver. 'It'll be a quiet house without him.'

Three other men had died at sea, or under a castle wall. Gretl's sweetheart had been struck by an arrow in Kintyre, and they had buried him there and built a cairn over him.

I have never seen such grief as on the face of little Gretl. Yet there were no tears, no cry of sorrow.

The plunder, I was told that day, was pitiful compared to the rich treasure brought home in former cruises—a few bronze plates and pewter cups, two casks of French wine (but a storm had loosened a stave of one and the red wine was laced with salt), a few bales of English wool.

'That's the last thing we need,' said Ingi the weaver-wife, 'wool. We had wool enough here to put winter coats on all the Orkneymen.'

The women mocked the crew as they straggled up to the hall, one after the other. The mockery was silent, the deadlier for lacking words.

Old Sweyn Asleifson looked as though he had gazed into the skull.

After these sea scarecrows had gorged themselves on ale and rabbit stew and grilled fish, Sweyn suddenly shouted, 'Where's the stone splitter, where's the gable cobbler from Buchan?'

I do not reply to insults.

But his old glittering eye was on me. 'What have you been doing all summer? I hired you to build a new hall here...'

'The four walls of the barn are built,' I

said. 'It needs the carpenter and his men to fit the roofbeams.'

'You'll be paid,' he said, 'when the work is done. Hall, barn, byres, stable...'

It was then that the slow murmur, the grave interweaving of a dozen voices, drifted through the open door.

Sweyn dropped the rabbit bone on his plate. His fingers shone with grease. 'What's that?' said he. 'I didn't know we had a new dovecot in Gairsay.'

One of the very old men told Sweyn about the monks' shipwreck in spring, and how the monks were living off the ebb and the crags, and how they were hoping to sail on north to Faroe or Iceland when they had patched their ship, but instead of patching their ship they were building some kind of a chapel down at the far shore, on the other side of the hill.

It is hard to know whether old Sweyn is really angry, or is he putting on an act to divert his people. (I'm inclined to think that most of the 'heroic men' I've known were, in their innermost recesses, timorous creatures, and that they forge for themselves a mask of bravery and recklessness—only put aside in the presence of children, and women whom they love, and maybe a priest at the death bed.)

'Monks from Ulster!' cried this terrible man. 'Living on my island since early summer... Eating my seafood and my wild birds' eggs... Have they offered to pay rent?... Do I actually hear what you're telling me, that those drones have the impudence to be building a house on my island, with stones from my shore?... I look forward to having a word with those psalm singers in the morning. Whole ship or broken ship, they'll leave Gairsay before the week's end...'

Then he roared to a woman to bring him another ale jug.

When that jug was half drunk, he laughed and sang. The poor wretches of vikings laughed feebly, the length of the table. A flush came on their grey faces. By the time the big jar was empty, Sweyn was shouting that they had had a magnificent cruise, one of the best ever. And the drunk sailors began to tell each other, and anyone else who would listen, what English seaports they had taken, and what Baltic ships they had sacked and sunk.

The women stood here and there about the hall with contemptuous faces.

Sweyn went lurching off to bed at midnight. His seamen snored with their heads down on the long board.

The women cleared the tables.

Next morning, Sweyn was up at sunrise. He stood at the door of the hall and looked out at the great ripening oat-field. His face shone, as if the bronze mask of the harvester had been put on him.

The vikings were all harvesters now. Sweyn allowed them another day to sober up. Then their sickles flashed in the sun, and they waded knee deep in the great golden earth surges.

The women and the old men and the children gathered and bound the waves of cut corn.

I sat alone up at the quarry. I thought of ways to escape.

I thought of my Isabel, standing among the richer stooks of the Mearns.

SEPTEMBER

Once the oat-field was cut—and it was a good harvest—the carpenter Hrut and I directed the shaping and fitting of the roofbeams on the new barn. Then the thatchers came with a great load of springy heather and rushes. Soon a clear winnowing wind blew across the threshing floor, and the granary lay ready for the gathered wealth of summer.

I stood there alone, that sunrise, looking at the work of my hands, the great barn. Then the old monk came to the door of the barn and made a cross with a bright hand, and went away again.

Late in the month the islanders held their Harvest Home feast.

It was a night of great celebration, both on account of a successful harvest and of the new barn: I must say, the barn stood there, among the witherings and fire hazards of the perishable buildings of Gairsay, like a steadfast rock.

As for the harvest feast, I have to say that after the first hour I remember little about it. I have no head for ale horns, especially when the strongest ale is laced with honey.

There was harp and horn, dancing, gorging of mutton bones and smoked trout, and great vauntings about the heroic voyages of the ancestors, and the settling and taming of the obdurate soil of Orkney. There at the top table sat old Sweyn, his face like a ruddy sunset, shouting here and there across the music and the loud banter... He called to me, 'You, stonemason, you've idled a whole year out. You'll stay in Gairsay till the work is finished. Next year I expect the big house to be finished, and the byres and stable. Don't expect an extra fee, either.'

I took a deeper draught of the mead than usual, to give me a courageous tongue against this arrogant man, and I remember nothing after that till next morning, when the women were clearing away the tables and the dogs were gnawing the ox bones.

I was lying alone against the barn wall. My skull was beating like a drum.

'Get out of the way of my broomstick,' said the woman Ragna. 'You idle drunkard!'

OCTOBER

Now that the men of Gairsay were home, in October, and harvest was in, the island began to move into its true rhythms.

The fishermen went out with lines and creels. The fowler and his boys went to the hill. Men began to stack the sheaves inside; the cattle were driven from the dwindling fields into the old byres; the sheep were fleeced. The blacksmith's anvil rang like a black bell. The saws of the carpenter and his apprentices rasped in the workshop.

The vikings had become men of peace again.

My quarrymen were restored to me. The old men drifted back to their fires, now the first frosts were in the air. 'Now, lads,' I said, 'we'll have to work hard, through blizzards and gales. Sweyn Asleifson has great ambitions for next year—a stone hall and workshops and outbuildings. Ten thousand stones will be needed. We'll have to open a new quarry, lads...'

(Privately, I decided I would not be in Gairsay next year. Let Sweyn Asleifson hire an architect from Bergen or Hamburg. It was a miracle-worker he wanted, not a talented master mason.)

Amid all this autumn work, the folk of Gairsay seemed to have quite forgotten the monks in their hidden part of the island. Also, it was a very stormy month.

Between two gales, though, I heard the murmur of Lauds.

NOVEMBER

November is the month of the dead.

It was the old woman Norna who brought news to the quarry that the old man Borg had died on the night: 'Shaken like a last leaf from the tree,' said Norna.

Old Borg had been merry company many a day in summer.

It astonishes me always, the tranquil way those old women bring news of a death, as if there was a certain satisfaction in an end having been achieved, a circle rounded out, a story told.

But the death celebrant had more.

'Per, the old shepherd, he died at the weekend. He went out to the shearing without his coat in that rainstorm...'

Old Per had handled a few hundred stones in the summer quarry, too.

'And', said Norna, 'I don't think old Svett will be here after midnight. He has the death look on him.'

My quarrymen turned away from the old shrouding-wife, as if she might utter one of *their* names.

Then Norna left.

'I always make a wide circle about that old creature,' said Paul who works the hoist in the quarry. 'She puts the shivers on me.'

'Go down to the shore,' Paul said later to one of the labourers, a young lad. 'Tell the Irish monks about three deaths.'

The boy was back soon. 'I told the chief bald-head,' he said. 'But he knew already. He would light candles, he said...'

Then the boy said the chapel was almost ready. The monks were putting a shell-sand mortar on. They were roofing it with driftwood and turf.

Sweyn (said the boy) had sent his carpenter to patch the monks' ship.

A great storm came from the northeast and blew the last leaves from the tree in the hall garden. The gale of death blew two more lives into darkness.

The hammers thudded and chisels chirped in the deep quarry. The levers and sling hauled out thousands of stones.

I spoke privately, down at the shore, to a fisherman from the Island of Horses. I paid him good silver, we whispered together. He was to come for me, the first fine day after Twelfth Night.

The fisherman said, 'The Irish bald-heads have left. Did you not know? I saw them sailing northwards, off Scabra in Rousay, yesterday...'

DECEMBER

The great darkness of the year.

Men and women came and went like shadows.

The only bustling place was the hall kitchen, where a score of women were preparing, over fires, the Yule feast. The huge ale cask murmured away in a corner.

Darkness and silence.

I was aware of the great silence, now that the monks had taken their eight-fold cluster of psalms away. But that had been, not sound, but a deeper purer silence...

Now the island was all shadows and whispers, on Yule eve.

I had decided that I would have no part in their feast. On the solstice, three days before, I had raised the question of my fee with Sweyn Asleifson. 'What fee? When the

285

work's done, next year, you will get your gold. That was the agreement...'

I had spent a whole year in this madhouse of an island for nothing!

I expect the old pirate knew that, once out of Orkney, I would never come back to build Langskaill, his new house.

I kept to my nook.

I got tired of throwing dice with Skarf and Brand, in the candle flicker. I wrote a few lovesick winter words to my Isabel.

I walked down to the shore one afternoon. What shadow stepped out of the small boat, and whispered an instruction to the boatman, and went cannily up the slippery ebb-stones to the hall?

I recognised the old bishop in the red of sundown.

What was Gulielmus Orcad the bishop doing in this pagan island, at Christmas? Surely he ought to be saying his High Mass in St Magnus in Kirkwall, or in the island of the martyr, Egilsay.

It was not a day to please wintered men, for the fast was being observed. The sullen shadows chewed bits of dried fish, and drank cups of cold water, indoors.

Sea stones rasped. Three fishing-boats were being hauled up. There would be no fishing till after Epiphany. Shadows of twelve fishermen trooped up from the shore.

I spoke to them. They passed me without a word, going on to the bothy.

The thousand building blocks, black with night, lay stacked at the quarry. A star flashed from a pool deep in the quarry.

I think this was the most wretched day I had spent in Gairsay.

I made a circuit of the hill in the darkness, and saw that Langskaill was empty too. The torches went out. The fires in the kitchen were damped down. It looked like Valhalla, hall of heroes, after the death of the gods.

Frost crackled audibly in the ruts and pools about the farm.

At midnight, Bishop William began to celebrate the Mass of the Nativity in the monks' shore stone church.

All the people of Gairsay were crowded into that sea-cold chapel. Everyone was there, from old Sweyn to the child who had chased butterflies all summer.

The voice of the bishop was grave and sweet as midnight approached. 'And Joseph also went up from Galilee to the city of David, to be enrolled with Mary his espoused wife, who was with child... There was no room for them in the inn.'

At last the old man took the bread and wine, fruit of the work of their hands, and offered it.

The lad who had mixed mortar for the new barn in July rang the bell.

Then, in purest silence, Christ came down among his people at midnight.

St Christopher

The ferryman stood in the stern of his boat and a man with a bag, a scroll and a seal with a lump of wax said, 'Ferry me to the island, man.' Christopher rowed the taxman to the island and held out his hand and said, 'One penny.' The taxman said, 'Official business. You'll be paid at the Martinmas term.'

The islanders saw the taxman on the beach and they went inside the crofts and barred the doors.

The harvest had been bad that year. The fishing had been poor.

An island girl stood on the shore. She said, 'I am going to be married tomorrow in the island with the blue hills. Will you sail me across?'

The ferryman said, 'No fare, no ferry.'

The girl said, 'The bridegroom's mother will give you an oatcake and honey, and a jar of ale at the fire, and a silver coin.'

The ferryman hoisted a sail and he ferried the bride to the Hoy shore. And the mother-in-law said, 'What honey?

What shilling? Come tomorrow to the wedding feast...' The bride laughed and gave Christopher a kiss.

Christopher said, sailing back to the noust of the island, 'I hope my wife doesn't smell the honey of that kiss when I sit down to have my dinner...' He was carrying back from Hoy a man with two panicky hoof-scattering sheep to sell at the Hamnavoe market. The shepherd threw the two burdens of wool and yammering foolishness among the seaweed. The ferryman said, 'Twopence—a penny for you and a ha'penny a sheep.'

The hillman said, 'I'll have money at night when I sell the ewes. I'll give you a dram in the Arctic Whaler then, and your twopence of course.'

A tramp and his wife and six bairns tried to climb aboard like shadows the time Christopher was bargaining with the Hoy shepherd. 'Get out,' said the ferryman. 'Get back to your ditch and your fire and your rabbit stew. Away with you, vagabonds, make pots and tin mugs like honest tinker folk.'

The tinker wife took from her rags a new kettle. 'This is for you, Chris,' said she. 'It's the bonniest kettle that scoundrel of a man of mine ever made. Sail us to

290

Scapa beach. We have a sackful of tin cups to sell in Kirkvoe.'

'Sit tight,' said the ferryman. 'Look at that purple cloud. There'll be rain and wind, there'll be big waves.'

The *Sea-goose* trod the crests and the troughs as far as Scapa. The sack of cans made a great din among the waves. The ragged kids sang all the way to Scapa.

'I hope Thomasina is pleased with the kettle,' said the ferryman, sailing a Kirkvoe merchant to Flotta to buy a beached whale; he had jars for the oil and salt to salt the whale steaks. The Kirkvoe merchant stood grey in the face on the Flotta shore, such sickness had throbbed through him.

'One penny,' said Christopher.

'You scoundrel,' cried the merchant of big fish. 'You were nearly the death of me. I'll give you a dozen tallow candles from this whale next time I see you in my shop in the Laverock of Kirkvoe.'

'Poor business today,' said Christopher. 'Thomasina will be pleased when I show her the day's takings.'

The merchant was blustering and bargaining among a dozen Flotta men, the guardians of the whale.

A spinster with spectacles and silver hair came down to the shore with a basket of knitted things. 'Please, row me to Hamnavoe to the draper's there. He has promised to buy my winter's work.'

'One penny,' said Christopher. 'But you should bide at home, Kitty. The storm's getting worse.'

'What do I care about storms?' said Kitty Corston, who had a sweetheart drowned twenty years ago. 'I have a new-knitted bonnet here to keep the sleet and spindrift out of your bonny hair, man. And a shilling when you sail me back in the morning.'

And the wind howled and the sea snarled all the way to Hamnavoe. And the basket of knitting smelt of clover and marigolds. And Kitty's bonnet kept the strong salt out of Christopher's hair.

Thomasina raged at him by lamplight for the stupidest poorest ineptest ferryman that ever dipped an oar. 'And soon,' cried she, 'we'll be poorer than the tinkers. The landlord will put us out on the street. The sheriff's officer will take your boat from you and sell it for debt...' She raged worse, Thomasina, beside the hearth fire, than the tempest outside.

In the midst of her raging, Christopher fell asleep in his chair.

Oh, the storm lasted all that night, and

was still at its bagpipes and drums and mad dances in the first light.

And the ferryman went down to his boat.

And there a small boy was waiting on the beach. Says the child to the boatman, 'Please sir, row me to the Island of Hunger out there. I have something for the hungry people.'

But the child had nothing in his hands. And the wind made tumults of his bright curls.

The shopkeepers were taking down their shutters in the street above, and down at the wave-washed slipways a fishwife, Maggo Sinclair, was swilling a basin of fish.

Maggo Sinclair threw two fish to the child. 'A bonnier bairn I never saw,' said Maggo Sinclair.

Guthrie the baker came out of his bakehouse with a tray of smoking loaves on his head. 'A small traveller like you should have a bite on a stormy morning,' said Guthrie (who was said to be a greedy man, and mean). 'Here's a few cookies for you...' And Guthrie put down his tray on the gull-shrieking cobbles and took five cookies from his batch and put them into a paper poke and gave them to the boy.

The boy said thank you very gravely to

Maggo the fishwife and to Guthrie the baker.

'I'm sorry to say,' said the ferryman, 'that we can't cross to the Island of Hunger today. The *Solan Goose* couldn't live in a storm like this.'

'Pax,' said the boy over the fishes and the loaves and the thundering havocking stone-grinding waves.

Christopher and his passenger sailed out from the piers, in fine blue weather, to the Island of Hunger.

The Sons of Upland Farm

1

A farmer on the island of Hoy had three sons.

His wife died in middle age. But Adam the farmer said, 'This farm has been in our family for six generations. I have seen it grow from a poor hill croft in my grandfather's time to the most fertile farm in the parish. Now it doesn't matter how soon I follow my wife into the kirkyard. There are three sons. The inheritance is secure.'

The farmer had a share in a ship that traded out of Hamnavoe in Orkney to the Baltic.

He said one day to William, the eldest son, 'I think you should sail in our ship *Heatherbell* on her next voyage. I don't altogether trust the skipper. The profits have been down for three voyages past. Keep an eye on the bills of lading and the waterfront exchanges. Then be back in time for harvest.'

His son William joined the ship at

Hamnavoe at mid-summer. He got on well with the skipper and the crew. Once the cargo of salted herring—two hundred barrels—was under hatches, the ship sailed with a fair wind and tide through Scapa Flow.

Neither ship nor crew was ever seen again.

It was known there had been an easterly storm in the North Sea, that had damaged many ships.

The *Heatherbell*, it seemed, had been lost with all hands.

2

The second son was called Jamie.

He was a hard-working young man and when he was still a boy he knew most things about work on a big farm. It was said he knew the 'horseman's word', that could make the most intractable horse gentle and biddable.

The farmer employed several farm servants, men and girls. He drove them hard—he sometimes struck one or other if they did something stupid or perverse—but he paid them a higher fee than the other farmers, and he saw to it that they were well fed and housed.

His sons he treated more roughly than

the servants.

He said one day to Jamie, 'I've bought a horse from a farm in Aberdeenshire. You're to go tomorrow to fetch the horse here. Don't delay by as much as one night. Here's your fare. They'll feed you at the farm in Aberdeenshire.'

The second son said there was to be a meeting of the island Horsemen's Society, and they were expecting him to help with initiations in the great Bu barn, the next night.

'You'll take the ferry south to Scotland,' said the farmer, 'in the morning.'

So Jamie set out from Hamnavoe.

The farmer expected son and horse back within the week. When a fortnight had come and gone, he began to be worried.

He wrote a letter to the horse-dealer, asking if his son Jamie had taken the horse, according to the bargain.

The horse-dealer sent no answer. (Horse-dealers in those days rarely put pen to paper. The spoken word, the struck hand, drams taken, the exchange of a few sovereigns—that was the only kind of communication they understood.)

But half a year later the farmer did get a letter, from Jamie. 'Dear Father, It might as the Good Book says be a good thing for the eyes to behold the sun, and young men are bidden to rejoice in their youth, but there has been little joy in your farm since our mother died, and the sun does not shine on your fields and labourers as it does on the oat-fields of other farmers. I write to say that I will not return to Hoy. The horse you bought is still with the dealer. I met in the Mearns a bonny kind lass, a tattie-picker from Ireland, and I have settled there with her and we are married and I am farm manager to a rich landlord who lives in London and attends the Parliament there.'

3

The farmer lit his pipe with this letter and said, 'Life gets more interesting the older you get. But you have to harden your heart like a stone. Tom, you'll have to sharpen *your* ideas, my lad. I'm grey and bent. There's the heavy burden of this farm on you in the years to come, and you with the wits of a scarecrow.'

Tom was the third son.

He was the strangest boy the island had known for a long time.

It was not that Tom was work-shy. He could do whatever he was told, such as dig peats or stumble after an ox at ploughtime, or sink creels for lobsters. But he could do nothing by himself. He had to be shown what to do, and then he did the work, not well, but passably. The prospect of him operating this big farm after his father was dust was unthinkable. It was very hurtful to the old man.

Tom was very good at imitating the songs of birds and all animal sounds. Half-way down a furrow, he would stop and speak awhile to the ox, like two friends conversing. But he was best of all at imitating the speech of the island folk, for everyone had a different way of speaking, and Tom had the tune and the rhythm of their talk to perfection. Everyone laughed except the person being imitated, who would generally be glum for a whole day after. (But this person had, always, done something to disrupt the harmony of the parish.)

But what good are bird calls and satire on a farm, especially a rich important farm like Upland?

The old farmer looked at his son and shook his head.

Next Lammas fair at Hamnavoe, all the farm workers in Hoy had the day off, as every year. They went in half a dozen skiffs to Hamnavoe, and Tom sailed with them. 'Keep an eye on the creature!' said the farmer. 'It wouldn't make that much difference if he disappeared, like his brothers. But still, a father needs some kin to close his eyes. I hope Tom finds some good hard-working country lass at the fair.'

When the six skiffs sailed back to Hoy in late evening, Tom wasn't there.

'There was a troupe of play-actors in Hamnavoe,' said the Hoy shepherd to the farmer. 'There was a hurdy-gurdy man and a man who threw burning knives all round a lass, and a monkey in a cage. They sang the latest London songs. It cost sixpence to get in. I didn't go. But I saw Tom going in. Tom wasn't at the pier when we foregathered at sundown to sail home. Maybe he fell asleep in the pub. He'll be home in the morning with a sore head.'

'I expect the play-actors have taken him for a side-show,' said the old farmer.

4

The next winter the farmer died.

Then slowly the farm went to pieces.

The farm servants feed themselves to other farms. A fourth cousin of the farmer, a Kirkwall solicitor the farmer had never once spoken to, claimed to inherit the land and stock and dwellings. At once he put them on the market.

But the islanders were chary of purchasing, for the lost sons might turn up some day, and demand their inheritance.

The farm remained unsold. Doors and shutters warped. The roofs began to fall in. The meadowland was full of rushes. Bad boys out for a lark on Hallowe'en night sent stones splintering through the windows, leaving black stars.

The rabbits made burrows under the ploughland.

The plough at the barn wall was flaky with rust, then that powerful share was completely eaten with the slow red fire.

5

The little hotel in the village twelve miles away closed its guest rooms in winter, once the English grouse-shooters and trout-fishers went home. Only the bar room stayed open for the convenience of the islanders.

A half-dozen men were drinking at the fire one bitter cold winter night.

Suddenly the door opened and three strangers came in, shaking snow from their capes. They set down their boxes and trunks.

The landlord was about to say his house was closed for the winter, when the huge foreign-looking man with the red beard and the ring in his ear rang three gold

sovereigns on the counter and requested
three rooms for the night.

A sovereign in those days was a large
fee.

The landlord put the coins in his till and
listened to the rich music it made among
the pennies and farthings.

Then the landlord opened his register
and the three guests signed, one after
another.

'Now, gentlemen,' said the landlord,
'what can I get you this cold night?'

The gruff red-beard who had signed
himself as 'Merchant and Shipowner' said,
'I hear they make good whisky among
the hills here. Bring three glasses of Hoy
malt.'

The strangers went over and sat by
themselves at the window seat. The
window was crammed with stars, until
the next snow shower blotted them out,
and after that the stars were out again, a
winter swarm in the deep purple.

The island men, after a silence, began to
discuss the island news, such as it was.

One said there had still been no legal
settlement about Upland Farm. It was a
sorrowful thing, to see a prosperous farm
in ruins.

A girl at the other end of the island—it
seemed—had been put out of the farm she
worked in, on account of 'her condition'.

The farmer had told her to go to the Inspector of Poor in the village. He might be able to give her a shilling or two to get by on, or direct her to the poorhouse in Kirkwall. To stay on as butter-and-cheese lass at his farm, he declared, was impossible.

The girl had knocked at this door and that, and been given a cup of milk or a scone, but no one had offered to take her in.

'Now,' said the landlord, 'I was having my afternoon snooze in the rocking-chair, when I thought I heard a knock at the door. But it must have been a snowfall from the roof, or the fire sinking.'

'Well,' said the shepherd, 'I saw that lass wandering across the hill after sunset. I called after her, she was welcome to bide at our fire. But a blizzard muffled my shout. When the blizzard passed, there was no one to be seen.'

'God help anybody out on a night like this,' said the blacksmith.

'Well,' said the shopkeeper, 'but they bring it on themselves.'

'Now, gentlemen,' said the landlord to the rich guests, 'my wife has a pot of good Scotch broth on the fire, and there's steak and clapshot, whenever you're ready.'

The black-bearded guest who had signed himself in as 'Landowner'—and a prosperous keeper of flocks and herds he seemed—said they had an errand to do first, then they would return for their supper, maybe after midnight.

'The roads are drifted under. Will I send the boy to go before you with a lantern?' said the landlord.

The youngest of the strangers, who had signed in as 'Poet', said they would find their way by the stars. 'When a child is born,' he said, 'there is one star kindled to light the soul on its journey...' The poet, unlike his two companions, was rather poorly clad for winter, in an old patched coat and moleskin trousers. Out of his pocket stuck a penny whistle. He was much the merriest of the three. But often he paused upon a thought, and then his gravity seemed to be a deeper pool than the austere looks of his companions.

They got to their feet, all three, at the same time.

'Might I ask, where exactly are the gentlemen bound for?' asked the landlord.

They said nothing. They shouldered their boxes. They walked out into a new flurry of snow.

'I think they're government men,' said the gravedigger. 'From the excise. You should never have sold them that home-made whisky.'

The landlord said he wasn't afraid of that.

They heard, between two surges of snow, a scatter of notes from the road-end. The third stranger, the poet, the patched one, was playing on his tin whistle.

'Look in the register,' said the shepherd. 'See what their names are.'

The names were William Adamson, James Adamson and Thomas Adamson, of Upland Farm in Hoy, Orkney.

It was near midnight when the heirs of Upland arrived at the ruined farm.

All was silence, darkness, desolation.

But in the byre where the cattle had wintered long ago, they saw a feeble light.

Someone had stuck a candle in an empty bottle.

It seemed to be earth's tremulous answer to the star of the Nativity.

One by one the travellers walked towards the glimmering cowshed.

The Road to Emmaus

The man was standing at the side of the road, with his hand held out.

'Pay no attention,' I said. It wasn't safe. The place was thick with spies and informers. I expected to be arrested at any moment.

Tom stopped the car beside the man. The sun was down and we couldn't see his face well. I opened the car door. 'Where are you going?' said Tom.

The man asked were we going anywhere near the village of Emmaus. Tom said we would likely be spending the night there, if we could get a room. The stranger got into the back of the car.

I didn't like it. The car jerked forward. For a couple of miles nobody said a word. We passed one farm where a couple of soldiers were speaking in the lighted doorway to an old farmer and his wife.

The man said, 'The countryside is not so quiet as I've seen it.'

'You can say that again,' said Tom.

'Are you from hereabouts?' I said.

'From further north,' said the man. 'But I know this place pretty well. I've never seen so many soldiers and police.'

'Haven't you heard?' said Tom. 'Where were you all last week? It's a lot quieter now than it was.'

'Shut it,' I said. I was worried about the man. He could easily have been an informer. Tom talks too much.

'What happened?' said the man.

'It was supposed to be an uprising,' said Tom. 'A coup. At the weekend.'

'That was the rumour,' I said. 'We don't know. It's got nothing to do with us.'

'Whatever it was,' said Tom, 'it was stamped out. The leader was shot. They shot him outside the town, on the side of that small hill. They got rid of two sneak-thieves at the same time. Shot all three of them. It was some spectacle.'

'It's all over now,' I said. 'The less said the better.'

'What about the man's followers?' said the man in the back seat. 'What happened to them?'

'Took to their heels,' said Tom. 'Hiding here and there. Such brave talk out of them a day or two before. They were going to do this and they were going to do that once they had the post office and the radio station.'

'We know nothing,' I said. 'This is just what we heard, what Tom's telling you.' (In fact Tom and I had been at all their meetings since the start of winter. That leader could make believers out of stones. He could make stones break into flower with that tongue of his. Tom and I and a few others joined the first night we heard him speak. What scared me now was that our names might be listed in the secretary's book, and somebody in authority might turn it up. These things didn't seem to worry Tom at all.)

'Are you sure he's dead?' said the man.

Tom turned round in the driving seat.

'Watch where you're going,' I said.

'Listen,' said Tom. 'I was there, in the crowd. So was Jimmy here. One thing the soldiers know how to do is shoot a man. Thousands of folk were there. It was a real holiday. A dozen vans at the foot of the hill selling sausages and beer. The military knows how to put on a good show.'

'What happened?' said the man.

'Listen,' I said. 'Get this clear. Tom and I, we don't know who you are. But we can't be too careful nowadays. We had nothing to do with this man. Tom's just telling you what we heard.'

'The cock crew,' said the man. 'Well, I'm interested.'

'He's all right,' said Tom to me. 'I can tell.'

And Tom said to the man, 'Jim here—he's my pal—he always plays it safe.' Tom laughed.

We drove on for another mile in silence. It was going to be a very dark night, with no stars.

'As a matter of fact,' said Tom, 'I was impressed with the leader the very first time I heard him. So was Jim here. I thought he had some marvellous ideas. He could have done something if he'd gotten the chance. Now he's dead.'

The man said, 'But his ideas are still there, in men's minds and imaginations. You can't get rid of them so easily.'

'That's true,' said Tom.

'It was all nonsense,' I said, 'from the start. We ought to have known. We were taken in by a spellbinder.'

'I'm still waiting to hear what happened,' said the man.

'What always happens,' said Tom. 'There was a traitor in the camp. One of the inner group, the secretary and treasurer. They got at him.'

'The secretary was right,' I said. 'He knew what would happen. There would be a rising. The army would put it down. Then the whole country would get it. He did right to nip it in the bud.'

'There wasn't much bloodshed,' said the man. 'That's good.'

'Just the leader,' said Tom. 'They shot him good and proper. They grilled him for

309

a whole night before. He was in a shocking state when they led him up the hill, the two bums trailing after him. Fancy that great one shot along with Fritz and Mac!'

'That doesn't signify,' I said.

'Well,' said Tom, 'that last night they were having some kind of consultation at a farm where they used to go a lot. The leader, you know, and the inner circle. A place just outside the town.'

'We weren't there,' I said.

'Things were at a crisis,' said Tom. 'There were rumours and stirrings everywhere. The town would support them, they were sure of it. It was just a question of when to strike. The leader went away by himself to think things through. They were arrested about midnight. The secretary led them right to the place. Of course it was only him they were interested in. They let the rest go. They were nonentities. They could be picked up anytime.'

'So much for his new order,' I said.

'They took him to the police first,' said Tom. 'He was passed between the inquisitor and the governor all night. The governor seemed to think it was all a bit of a joke. The inquisitor threatened to go over the governor's head. Finally the governor gave in, washed his hands of the whole business. He handed the leader to the political police. You know what happens to anybody who spends time in that company.'

'They roughed him up,' I said.

'We weren't like some of them,' said Tom. 'At least we stayed in the city. We wanted to see what would happen. The big fisherman, he had guts. He actually got into the inquisitor's courtyard. He was there all that night.'

'He was recognised too,' I said.

'A rising,' said the stranger. 'Maybe another kind of rising was meant.'

'Maybe,' I said. 'It was hard to tell sometimes just exactly what he meant.'

There was a roadblock ahead, and three soldiers. They signalled us to stop.

The corporal shone his torch inside the car. He held the beam a long time in the stranger's face. I was scared to look round, or to say or do anything. 'This is it,' I thought.

'OK,' said the corporal. 'Drive on.'

Tom's as cool as a cucumber. He drove fast and steady. We had about ten miles to go. When I opened my cigarette packet my hands were shaking.

'He'll know me the next time he sees me,' said the stranger.

The man's voice had a peculiar quality. It was like a voice that you remember from years back, of someone in authority—a teacher maybe, or a priest. But there was a thickness and a darkness in it, as if it was trying out a second language. And it was quiet, as if there was a meaning deeper than the thing said. I wondered how his face would look in the sunlight. And yet I would have been more glad if he had just got out of the car and walked away.

'Suppose', he said, 'that this coup had taken place, and been successful...'

'How could it—it was all tommy-rot,' said Tom. 'To bust the most disciplined army the world has ever seen—us, a rabble of tradesmen. Thinking about it, now, it's almost laughable.'

'But just suppose,' said the man, 'that there was a new governor up there in the palace, a patriot, an able and a just ruler, one long expected. That would have called for flags and trumpets. But how long would it last? Death puts an end to the ablest and best of men. Then the bad times come back.'

'Yes,' I said. 'That's where we were doubly gulled. There was no question of history. The new regime was to last for ever. It was all in the books, the political theorists. For ever and ever. That's what excited us so much. We were fools.'

'Well,' said Tom, 'I was telling you. The police roughed him up. I didn't recognise him on the hillside. He looked like he had been dragged behind a car for miles.

Jimmy and I, we were in the crowd.'

'Some leader,' I said.

'They stood him up against a rock,' said Tom. 'Him and the two bums. The sergeant offered them all a noggin. Fritz and Mac knocked theirs back at once. The leader shook his head. Fritz had taken his rum so fast he had sloshed most of it into his beard. Somebody in the crowd shouted, "Hi, Leader, how about making a run for it? We can postpone the kingdom till tomorrow..." There was some laughter at that. Then Mac turned on the leader and cursed and ranted, as if he was to blame for all their troubles. Fritz seemed to be put out by that. You know, he's one of them miserable bums too low to think about. Anyway, he said to the leader, "Pay no attention, brother. You're a good guy." And the leader smiled at him, if anybody can smile whose mouth and eyes are a pulp. All this time, of course, the firing squad are loading up their guns and shuffling their feet in the dust. Then a lance-corporal put a cigarette into the mouths of the men going to be shot and lit them. There was no hurry.'

'The leader didn't take a cigarette,' I said.

'That's right,' said Tom. 'He didn't. Mac choked on the smoke and coughed and coughed. A soldier had to hit him hard on the back. The leader, he looked quite at his ease, apart from his bruises and all the blood on him. "Right," said the sergeant, "bandage their eyes."

' "I haven't finished my fag," said Fritz indignantly.

' "Cheer up," said the leader when their eyes were being bandaged. "This is the greatest thing that's ever happened to you or Mac or anybody."

'Fritz, blindfolded now, nodded seriously in his direction. Then suddenly, to the disgrace and shame of everybody, Mac began to blubber for his mother. (The poor woman, he must have broken her heart when he was still in short trousers.)

'The sergeant held up a handkerchief. The eight guns levelled. Mac was still whimpering. The leader gave a shout. It was like the cry of somebody who had succeeded just when everything seemed to be in ruins. The hankie fluttered down. The guns split the hillside apart. The three of them grew rigid. Their chests were torn open. They sagged and slumped into the dust. The echoes of the guns were still wandering about in the distant hills. Then the sergeant took a pistol out of his belt and put a last shot into each of them.'

'That's right,' I said. 'Tom and I, we saw it all.'

'You tell a good story,' said the man.

'Thank you,' said Tom. 'Then the crowd began to disperse. The fun was over for that day. Jim here and me, we hung on for a bit to see what would happen. A lorry drove up and soldiers got out and threw Mac and Fritz in the back. They didn't even cover them up. I suppose they took them to the paupers' cemetery. But they didn't move the leader. There he lay under the sun. Some of the women who used to hang around the group, they had been there all the time. They kept edging closer to the body. You know how it is, they weren't sure of the position. They could have got into trouble. There were three or four of them. Sometimes they would be still for minutes on end. Then a stir would go through them. They moved about each other. It was like a kind of slow sorrowful dance. And every movement took them closer to the dead leader. Then I saw his own mother there among them. I never felt so sorry for anybody.'

'A pity for her,' I said. 'She's a good woman.'

'Finally,' said Tom, 'the women were all standing round him. Then, slowly, one by one, they sank on their knees. Then the mother lifted him by the shoulders and smoothed his hair. It was very touching, that. It was the way she would have comforted him many a time when he was a kid and maybe had fallen and bruised his brow.'

'The soldier on guard paid no attention to the women,' I said. 'He must have been told.'

'That's right,' said Tom. 'Just before sunset a smart van drove up, and a man got out who used to attend the meetings too. I forget his name. He's got plenty of gilt and a fine old house in the country. That's all we knew about him. He wasn't in the inner circle, you know, but he was well respected in the party. First he looked down at the leader, then he went up to the soldier on guard and showed him a letter. The soldier studied it, then nodded his head. Three men got out of the van. They threw a sheet over the leader and rolled him up in it. Then they carried him into the back of the van. Two of the women started to cry then.'

'Not the mother,' I said. 'You could see she was pretty low, but she didn't utter a sound.'

'Then this rich guy got into the driving seat and they drove off. They'd have buried him up at his villa. Some of them posh places have vaults, you know, where the dead lie for hundreds of years, all embalmed, as flushed and fresh as if they were having a sleep.'

'That's right,' I said. 'I've heard that too.'

The stranger, after a time, began to speak, almost as if he was speaking to himself, about the kingship of every man, or something like that, that I couldn't follow. But anyway, this little kingdom doesn't last long, seventy years or so. (I smiled to think of Tom and me being little kings.) And always this kingdom is beset by 'the seven rebel barons'. Somehow, in spite of them, he has to plough and sow his fields, and bring his harvest in. (King Tom and King Jim, we're bookies' runners, and our harvest fluctuates.) At last he invites his friends to break bread with him in his great farm, and there are guitars and dancing and booze till first light.

At this point, I must have dropped off, and no wonder, I had hardly closed an eye for three nights. What I dreamed was this voice, saying words: there was nothing but a voice, and it went in a kind of slow song, like the church bells I used to hear when I was a kid, far off. The song was only a whisper to begin with, in darkness, and all it did was name things, like 'star' and 'sea' and ordinary things like that, and it was like I was getting to know the things for the first time, and I was delighted with them, for some reason, in the dream. Well, what's so special about 'trees' and 'stones', words like that? The voice rose from a whisper to be a kind of a low chant, and then every word was accompanied by music, like flutes and guitars and drums. It was strange, right enough. I wouldn't be telling this at all, but I've never heard music like the music I heard in Tom's car, in this dream I was having. Never. 'Star', it began, a whisper. Then 'sun and moon'. Then 'hill and sea'. Then 'plant', and it seemed like oak trees, roses, and apples were there, all shaken into life by the song. I was aware in the dream of a blade of corn and a bunch of grapes. 'Insect', and I was delighted with bees and spiders (I tell you this, I'm scared of spiders, always have been, I *hate* the things). 'Bird' went the music, and there were hundreds of wings, eagles and blackbirds and doves. I didn't see them, only I knew they were there, in the dream, more real than they'd ever been, and I knew that a pigeon was sitting in a certain tree—not that I could see a thing. 'Fish'. A whale came surging up out of the sea, a salmon leapt at a waterfall, there was a little drifting fish so small no eye could possibly see it. 'Animal'. A lion was there, burning like the sun, and a wolf, and a white shivering lamb. I knew they were glad to be all together in the same place, though as I say I didn't see a thing, only the word 'animal' and the music that went with it... 'Man'—I don't know how to put this, but the word was sung with a kind of wonderment (if you know what I mean) and joy, yes, but anxiously too. The creature was beautiful—you must forgive me for using words like 'wonderful' and 'beautiful', but it was sort of like what a kid feels on Christmas morning, only a lot more exciting. And all of the things named were part of this song. But, all of a sudden, so it seemed, but I know thousands of years had passed, something went wrong. The music died away. The light ebbed, till it seemed to be darker than it was in the beginning. I felt a terrible fear. Through the darkness and the silence I knew that the eyes of the creatures were glaring at each other. The song became the sound of an axe at a tree. I knew that a man was cutting down the first tree. Thud-thud went the axe, then the tree crashed down, then a saw rasped and rasped, there were shouts, I knew that a gallows was being made, I heard a chinking of nails. Then nothing but darkness and silence, till the voice sang, 'It is the end...' And then I woke up in a sweat... And Tom and the stranger were talking to each other as if I didn't exist, and Tom so deep in the discussion he was looking over his shoulder more than he was keeping his eye on the road. 'Clay,' Tom was saying, 'that's what

I think a man is. Clay with a breath or two and a pulse in it. Time dries the clay slowly, a wind comes and blows the dust away. And that's that...'

'No,' said the stranger, 'but in the kingdom I've been talking about the dust is smitten with a glory, like a cornfield at harvest time...' What can anyone make of talk like that?

I could see Tom was impressed, though, in spite of what he'd said. He drove on slowly, shaking his head now and then.

The village was in darkness. Curfew started at nine o'clock. Tom stopped the car in the square and we got out, the stranger too. 'Not much point in you going further tonight,' said Tom to the dark figure beside us. 'Jim and I know this good place to stay. You get supper and a comfortable bed. We'd be glad of your company.'

Tom should have spoken for himself.

Mrs Robinson was at home. She took a long while to answer our knocking. She was scared like everybody else. When she opened the door she was holding a candle. There must have been another power cut. She smiled when she saw Tom's homely face.

'Of course,' she said. 'Come right in. There's not another guest in the place. Three rooms. You'll want a bite of supper,

320

I know. The police are just everywhere. There were two of them here earlier. I'm surprised at you, Tom, and you too, Jim, travelling at a time like this.'

'We just wanted some peace and a good supper,' said Tom.

The dining room was lit with candles too. It was like we were three shadows in a silent congregation of shadows. We sat round a small table. I brought out my paperback and began to read by a candle flame. I closed my ears against the stranger. He and Tom were still talking, their heads inclined towards one another. I caught fragments of their jargon—'Kingdom' and 'the defeat of death' and 'the one dust that is man and bread and the earth, grave and golden corn'.

Mrs Robinson came in with bread and fruit and cheese and a bottle of wine, the supper she knew we liked.

'Now, gentlemen,' she said, 'make yourselves entirely at home. I don't think the police will bother us tonight.'

I laid down my novel.

'Well,' said Tom, 'we'll begin.'

We waited for the stranger to put his hand in first. The light of the candles laved his serious smiling face. I honestly didn't recognise him. He took a roll and broke it. As he did so his coat fell open and I could see the red seals and furrows across his throat and chest where the bullets of the executioners had gone in.

The Fight in the Plough and Ox

1

The farmers in the parish were peaceable men, and they drank on market days in an alehouse, the Plough and Ox kept by a lady called Madge Brims.

The fishermen's pub was called the Arctic Whaler. There the fishermen drank when they came in cold from the lobster fishing.

The men from the farms—the ploughmen and the shepherds—got on quite well with the fishermen. They met and mingled on the Hamnavoe street at the weekends, and sometimes exchanged a few bantering words. Once or twice a fight threatened, when the young ones fell to arguing, mostly about girls; but then the older men would come between the spitters and snarlers, and patch things up, and there was rarely ill-feeling.

But the country men never darkened the door of the Arctic Whaler, nor did the lobster men stand outside the door of Madge Brims's, the wall of which was studded with horseshoes, and think for one moment of going in there for a glass of Old Orkney whisky, price threepence.

The men from the land and the men from the sea segregated themselves strictly, when it came to refreshments at the end of a day's hard work.

In the Arctic Whaler, you would hear talk of smuggled tobacco from a Dutch ship, whales, halibut so big they broke the nets, shipwrecks, seal-women.

There was none of that kind of talk in Mistress Brims's—it was all about horse and ox, the best way to train a sheepdog, oats and barley, whether it was better to grind one's own grain or to take it in a cart to the scoundrel of a miller. Often, of course, the young men spoke about the lasses. The bonniest lass in the parish that year was said to be Jenny of Furss, the one daughter of a very poor crofter called Sam Moorfea of Furss. Sam was so poor he couldn't even afford to drink in Madge's place, where the ale was a penny the pewter mug. Sam Moorfea had to sit beside the fire at home and drink the ale he brewed himself, poured out for him by his beautiful daughter Jenny.

'Oh, but she's a right bonny lass, Jenny!' said Will the blacksmith who, by reason of his calling, always drank with the farm men. 'I would like well to have Jenny take me a mug of buttermilk, every day when I stand wiping sweat from me between the forge and the anvil.'

'No, Jenny deserves better than that,' said John Greenay, whose father owned a big farm. 'I can see Jenny with her arms full of sheaves at harvest time, and her long hair blowing brighter above them in the wind.'

The young countrymen seemed to vie with each other, that summer, in praise of Jenny Moorfea. Their faces shone with joy and beer. The old men shook their heads in the hostelry, as much as to say, '*We* thought that way once, too, before the sweet-mouthed lasses we married began to nag and rage at us...' They winked at each other, the old men. 'Ah well, but they'll find out in time, the young fools that they are...'

2

It so happened that Sam Moorfea had such a poor croft, and three young boys to feed, that he kept a small fishing-boat on the beach, and fished inshore for haddocks whenever he had a moment to spare from ploughing and threshing. His wife was six years dead, and so Jenny did all the housework and brought up

325

her three brothers well, and whenever her father caught a basket of fish, Jenny took them to Hamnavoe to sell to the housewives there.

And so, Jenny got to know the fishing folk well too. And that summer, when Jenny had arrived at her full beauty, some of the young fishermen looked at her, and they thought they had never in their lives seen such a lovely creature.

That first night, in the Arctic Whaler, the young men's talk was all of Jenny of Furss. 'My grandfather,' said Tom Swanbister, 'saw a mermaid on the Kirk Rocks and he was never done speaking about her beauty, but—poor old man—he died without setting eyes on Jenny Moorfea...'

'I'm saving up for a new boat,' said Alec Houton, 'I have twelve sovereigns now in the jar in my mother's cupboard. I would pour them singing into Jenny's hands for one kiss...'

Stephen Hoy said, 'I'm going to call my new boat *Jenny*. I was going to call her the *Annie* after the lass next door, that I thought I might marry some day. But now I've settled for *Jenny*. I'll get good catches with the *Jenny*.'

There was a young shy fisherman called Bertie Ness. At the mention of the name *Jenny*, a look of purest joy came on his face. But he said nothing.

The old fishermen at the bar counter shook their heads and turned pitying looks on the young fishermen. They had thought things like that too, in their youth, and they were still poor men, and they were nagged and raged at when they came in from the west with half-empty baskets.

3

It happened that year, that there was a very good harvest in Orkney, the most bountiful for twenty years. Even the poor croft of Furss was studded with golden stocks.

It was far otherwise on the sea. From horizon to horizon, the sea was barren. It seemed that the lobsters had gone in their blue armour to fight in distant underseas wars. It seemed that haddock and cod had been drawn by that enchantress, the moon, to far-away trystings.

It was a very hard hungry summer along the waterfront of Hamnavoe.

Week after week the boats returned empty from the west, to the shrieking of gulls and the mewling of cats and—worse—the tongue-tempests of the womenfolk.

No wonder it drove the men, after sunset, to the Arctic Whaler, where they sat silent and brooding for the most part.

One evening Stephen Hoy and Alec Houton quarrelled with each other in the Arctic Whaler as to which of their boats could sail further west. It began mildly enough, but soon they were snarling at each other. Other fishermen, young and old, joined in the dispute, voices were raised, old half-forgotten ancestral disputes were aired; it reached such a stage of anger that Walter Groat the landlord told them all to leave, get out, come back when they had some money to spend (for lately they had been sitting at the tables till midnight over one mug of thin beer, all they could afford.)

Out they trooped, like sullen churlish chidden dogs. The old men went home to their many-worded wives. The young men drifted by twos and threes along the street. At last they found themselves outside Madge Brims's hostelry. Inside, merry rustic voices were raised. Tomorrow was Harvest Home; they were getting into good voice for it.

The young fishermen did a thing never heard of before: they entered the tavern of the hill men, the farmers, the shepherds.

A sudden silence fell. It was as if a troop of wretched penniless outcast beachcombers had trooped up from the shore, bringing the coldness of the ebb with them—and that was pretty much the way things stood that night, in fact, with the fishermen.

But soon the country men returned to their drams and their stories and their loud bothy songs.

One or two went so far as to walk across to where the bitter fishermen stood against the wall and give them a welcome. Will the blacksmith offered to buy them all a dram. 'You look that miserable,' he said.

The fishermen looked at him coldly.

'Can I do anything for you gentlemen?' said Madge Brims to the young men from the salt piers. They answered her never a word.

From then on, the boys from the farms, the crofts, and the sheepfolds ignored those boors of fishermen.

They began to talk about girls. It was the high mark of every discussion or debate or flyting or boasting in Madge Brims's hostelry—it was inevitable it ended up with praise of bonny lasses.

At last John Greenay, son and heir of the wealthiest farmer in the parish, his face flushed like sunset with whisky, said, 'We all know fine who is the bonniest lass hereabouts, and that's Jenny Moorfea of Furss. And now I'm going to tell you men something—I'm going to marry Jenny in October. I'm going to take her home to Netherquoy. She'll be mistress there, some day.'

Hardly was the last boastful word out of his mouth than it was silenced by the impact of a pewter mug. The mug had been seized from a table by Stephen Hoy the fisherman and hurled with full force.

And at the same time Alec Houton yelled 'You yokel! You dung-spreader! Jenny Moorfea is coming to our pier to be my wife!'

A trickle of blood came from John Greenay's split lip. The pewter mug rolled about on the flagstone floor, clattering. That was the only sound to be heard for fully five seconds.

Then the young farm men leapt to the defence of their companion. They didn't like John Greenay all that much—he boasted overmuch about his gear and goods—and besides, they loved Jenny Moorfea more than he did (or so they supposed). But those young fishermen had challenged and insulted the whole race of farmers.

It was the worst fight ever known in a Hamnavoe hostelry since the days of the whaling men a century before. There was a flinging and thudding of fists—there were shouts of rage, contempt, fear, and pain—glasses splintered against the wall—heavy pewter mugs rang like armour on the stone floor—noses were broken, eyes looked like thunder clouds. Will Laird the blacksmith spat out a tooth. Hands closed about throats. There was the flash of a fishing knife. A table was knocked over and twelve glasses and mugs and a half bottle of Old Man of Hoy whisky fell in ruins.

It was the knife-flash that finally unlocked the petrified mouth of Madge Brims. 'Police!' she shouted from the open door of her hostelry. 'Help! Murder! My walls arc splashed with whisky and beer and blood!'

What did our heroes care about the law and disturbance of the Queen's peace? The shouts of battle grew louder. It seemed, in fact, as if an element of joy had entered into the affray. Frankie Stenhouse the young shepherd kicked the sea knife out of Ronald the fisherman's hand. It was to be a fair fist-fight—no heart-stabbings—no hangings for murder.

And still the wounded fighters (for not one of them now but had a broken nose or a thunder-loaded eye or a fractured jaw) melled bloodily on the floor, and raged louder against each other (with, it seemed to some, a mounting access of joy and delight).

Madge Brims had abandoned her tavern to go to the police station in the south end of Hamnavoe, a mile away, to summon the solitary policeman, Constable Bunahill.

A cunning lazy rogue of a fisherman, Simon Readypenny, seized his chance when the battle was at its height to slip behind the counter and put a bottle of brandy into one sea pocket and a bottle of Jamaica into another. And he disappeared into the night, leaving the tumult and the shouting to the fools. (He was found, grey in the face, in a cave, the next morning.)

The tumult and the shouting! It had now reached such a pitch that it could be heard in the granite houses of the respectable merchants and magistrates at the back of the town; and the shopkeepers got out of their beds and double-locked their doors. Indeed, a Graemsay man claimed to have heard the din in his island across Hoy Sound.

Then, a sudden silence fell.

The combatants disengaged themselves. They got to their feet, they made some semblance of wiping the blood from their faces with their shirt sleeves. Will Laird the blacksmith took a splinter of a whisky glass out of his beard.

They would not look at each other. They shuffled their feet like naughty boys chidden by the headmaster.

They were all on their feet now, in the wrecked hostelry, except young Bertie Ness the fisherman, whose kneecap had been cracked by a random kick.

The warriors had become aware of a presence in the pub door. All the snarling heads had turned at once. Jenny Moorfea of Furss was standing there, looking lovelier than any of them had ever seen her before.

Jenny Moorfea pushed her way through the wounds and the dishevelment, and she knelt down beside Bertie Ness, the stricken one, the poorest of all the poor fishermen there, and she kissed him.

4

That is all that needs to be said about the celebrated battle in Madge Brims's bar.

Six men—three from the farms, three from the fishing-boats—appeared at the Burgh court the following week and were fined half-a-crown each for disturbing the peace.

Then all six of them went from the courthouse into a neutral bar and pledged each other like battle-scarred comrades.

The following April, Jenny and Bertie Ness were married in the kirk.

They rented a little house at the end of a stone pier. Bertie Ness went to the fishing to begin with, with Stephen Hoy in his new boat, the *Annie*.

They had such good fishing that summer, and for the two succeeding summers, that Bertie was able to buy a secondhand fishing-boat for himself, the *Madge Brims*, and also to buy their cottage.

Now they have three children, and the two boys are as winsome as their mother, and the youngest—the daughter—is a delight to all the folk that live along that waterfront.

This Large Print Book for the Partially sighted, who cannot read normal print, is published under the auspices of

THE ULVERSCROFT FOUNDATION